# Worthy
## of Love

## ANDRE FENTON

DISUARD

FORMAC PUBLISHING COMPANY LIMITED
HALIFAX

Formac Publishing Company Limited recognizes the support of the Province of
Nova Scotia through the Department of Communities, Culture and Heritage. We
are pleased to work in partnership with the Province of Nova Scotia to develop
and promote our cultural resources for all Nova Scotians. We acknowledge the
support of the Canada Council for the Arts, which last year invested $153 million
to bring the arts to Canadians throughout the country. This project has been made
possible in part by the Government of Canada.

Cover design: Tyler Cleroux
Cover image: Shutterstock

---

Library and Archives Canada Cataloguing in Publication

Fenton, Andre, 1995-, author
     Worthy of love / Andre Fenton.

Issued in print and electronic formats.
ISBN 978-1-4595-0548-3 (softcover).--ISBN 978-1-4595-0549-0 (EPUB)

     I. Title.

PS8611.E57W67 2018                    jC813'.6                    C2018-902581-6
                                                                  C2018-902582-4

---

Published by:                Distributed in Canada by:      Distributed in the US by:
Formac Publishing            Formac Lorimer Books           Lerner Publisher Services
Company Limited              5502 Atlantic Street           1251 Washington Ave. N.
5502 Atlantic Street         Halifax, NS, Canada            Minneapolis, MN, USA
Halifax, NS, Canada          B3H 1G4                        55401
B3H 1G4                                                     www.lernerbooks.com
www.formac.ca


Printed and bound in Canada.
Manufactured by Marquis in Montmagny, Quebec, Canada in
December 2018.
Job #164344

*For those I love.*
*This is for you.*

# CHAPTER 1

# What Is He Eating?

It's always an awkward question, no matter the context. I mean, I wonder if the person asking ever feels like they shouldn't ask — it's a need to know thing. So I was a tad confused, not really sure why everyone in this room needed to know how much I weighed. It was the beginning of the school year, and we were in Gym class. Mr. Stephens, the teacher, had us come into the weight room in groups of fives to "See where we're at," as he put it. The school's new wellness policy required health check-ins during gym class. Every student had a file that held information about their height, weight, eye colour, hair colour and so on. I really wasn't a fan of stepping on a scale and revealing how much I weighed, though. I was with a group of five that included myself, Donny, Lewis, Matthew, and Tyler.

"All right," Mr. Stephens announced. "Donny, you hit the scale first."

"Whatever," Donny said.

Donny was a childhood friend of mine. We grew up together in the North End of Halifax. We were like brothers — though time sometimes put distance between us. He would hang out with the more rebellious teens while I was somewhere in between the shy kid who stood against the walls at school dances and the nerd who sat by himself during lunch. But at least I was brave enough to go to a dance, right?

Donny stepped on the scale. He had much longer hair and darker skin than I did. He was also in great shape but didn't do a lot with it. Mr. Stephens would often hassle him to play football, and Donny would always ignore him. Donny was more of an artistic guy but not pretentious. He was the most humble, genuine guy I knew.

The numbers on the electronic scale went from zero pounds to 193 pounds.

"Not bad," Donny said as he stepped off.

"Lewis, you're next." Mr. Stephens pointed.

Lewis was an asshole. I hated that guy. He was seventeen, a year older than all the other students in the room. He was held back a year. Now he was in class with us. It wasn't glamorous for him, so he spent most of his time making my life a living hell like it was his hobby. He was what most girls would call a douchebag. I wasn't brave enough to say it out loud.

Lewis gave Mr. Stephens a sneer with his stupid face and stepped on the scale with his chubby frame, shaved head, and pale skin. It went from zero pounds to 220 pounds.

"Hmm . . ." Mr. Stephens took note of that in his book.

"Yo, what was that 'hmmm . . .' about, Mr. Stephens?"

"It means we have work to do," he replied.

"Work on *me*? What about that fatass over there?" Lewis pointed my way.

Those words were like blades. I wasn't a fan of being called a fatass, but I couldn't respond and show weakness. That's what he'd want.

"That's enough, Lewis." Mr. Stephens shook his head.

"No. No, it's not," Lewis continued. "How much do you weigh, Adrian?"

I didn't say anything. I didn't know what to say.

"Enough to knock your dumb ass over," Donny intervened.

"Boys. Enough!" Mr. Stephens yelled. "I have six other groups of students to do this with, and I'm not going to be here all day with your petty crap."

He took a breath. "With that being said, do you want to go next, Adrian?"

"Sure," I muttered, not really wanting to. But I also wanted to get it over with. I stepped closer to the scale, walking past Lewis's stupid grin. I didn't want to do it. I really didn't. I put one foot forward and the other followed. Next thing I knew, both feet were planted and the numbers on the scale went from zero pounds to 280 pounds.

"Ha!" Lewis yelled from behind me. I shut my eyes. I knew there was going to be an insult, but it was overshadowed by a question. It was a question from Mr. Stephens.

"Adrian, what are you eating?" he asked in a voice of disgust.

I didn't reply. I turned around and ran out of the weight room. I felt ashamed of myself. I shouldn't have had to disclose my weight to a room full of people — it felt so wrong. I didn't want everyone in the school knowing how much I weighed. Anxiety made itself at home inside of me, so I had to leave. Outside, there were other students waiting for their turn in the weight room. I walked past all of them with my head down. Two hundred and eighty pounds of fat — I felt gross.

That afternoon, during our lunch hour, I sat with Donny in the cafeteria. He had a mouthful of sandwich while talking to me.

"Yeah, man. Lewis is full of crap. Don't pay any mind to him. He's a loser."

"I know," I said while taking my lunch out of my backpack. I had an egg sandwich. It was the type of food you could smell from halfway across the cafeteria.

"I got your back. If he messes with you, then he'll have to go through me."

Donny always felt like he had to play the big brother role for me. He kind of was, but if it came to violence or getting in trouble, I knew he would receive a harsher punishment than me. Because he was darker than I was, people saw him as more "dangerous," when in reality, he was a big, soft goofball. Violence wasn't really something I planned for when dealing with Lewis.

"Thanks, Donny, but I think everything will be fine. I don't want you to get in any trouble."

It was like I jinxed myself because as I said that, Lewis made his way into the cafeteria with that stupid grin on his face. He peered over at me from the entrance and made his way toward us.

"There's that asshole," Donny said under his breath.

Before I knew it, Lewis was right there in front of us. I knew it was going to be bad. I knew it was going to be embarrassing. I just wanted to shout, "Leave me alone!" But I didn't.

"What's up, Adrian?" he grinned at me.

"Dude, get out of here," Donny began.

"I'm not talking to you," Lewis shot back.

"Well I'm talking to you." Donny stood up.

The tension was pretty high. They weren't fans of each other.

"Lewis, leave my guy alone. I'm not messing with you," Donny continued.

I sat there, not knowing what to do or say, then suddenly I looked at my sandwich and I saw Lewis sticking his finger right through the top and down the bottom.

"Hey, what are you doing?" I demanded.

"It's not like you need that anyway, fatass," Lewis sneered at me. "You're almost three hundred pounds!" He said it loud enough for the entire cafeteria to hear. As soon as he said it, my heart sank into my stomach. I could see students eyeing me. I could feel their whispers lingering around me, and I felt sick. It felt like my biggest secret was now an open one.

"You're such an asshole, Lewis," Donny growled.

"Aha." Lewis laughed his stupid laugh.

That was when I snapped. I tore the sandwich from under Lewis's hand and flung it at him.

"What the hell!" he yelled. Gobs of egg covered his cheeks. I could hear laughs from around the cafeteria.

It didn't take long for Lewis to get the food off of his face. That was when he threw his fist into mine. I honestly hadn't known what to expect, but a bruised eye wasn't it. I hit the ground. Hard. All I heard was a collective gasp from the rest of the students. That was what humiliation felt like. It wasn't great.

I looked up to see Donny jump across the table at Lewis. They started fighting. Throwing fists full of anger back and forth as everyone in the cafeteria chanted, "Fight! Fight! Fight!"

Security soon came in and broke them up. Once that happened, I ran out of the cafeteria both hurt and embarrassed. I just wanted to go home. I grabbed my belongings from my locker and fought back tears. I couldn't cry, I couldn't let myself be weak, so I hid my misery and made my way home.

I was home before my parents so I had time to think of an explanation for the bruise on my face. I went straight to the bathroom and looked at myself in the mirror. It looked pretty bad. I had a huge red mark under my left eye. I couldn't let that happen again. I couldn't let Lewis bully me over my weight, I couldn't allow myself to be his punching bag, and I couldn't let my parents see me being beat up.

It's weird being bullied by a white kid when you're black. Well, half black. Both my parents were half black, so that gave me two halves. I was brown enough to be considered not white. Being bullied by someone who was white often felt racial, but that was something I was afraid to say out loud. I went to my bedroom and grabbed the stash of chocolate bars in my desk. There were two of them. I wasn't hungry, but I was stressed, and I ate them. Food was very relaxing, but that was my problem. It was *too* relaxing — 280 pounds too relaxing. I had a difficult relationship with food. I knew I should have cut back on what I ate, but being at school and being bullied by Lewis had taken everything out of me. Food was safety, security. It made me feel full when I felt lonely.

"What are you going to do, Adrian?" I asked myself while lying in my bed with a full stomach.

Shortly after I had said this, I heard cheering from somewhere. It was coming from my parents' room. I went to investigate the noise and realized that my dad must have left the TV on while I was at school. There was a mixed martial arts event on TV, and I heard an announcer almost falling out of his seat as he spoke.

"Matt Burner knocked out his opponent in the first thirty seconds of round two!"

I'd always liked martial arts. There was something beautiful in the discipline. I couldn't quite put my finger on it, but it was pretty wonderful to watch. The fighters were always in such great shape, too. It made me wonder if it might be a good way to lose weight. In the past, my dad would watch documentaries of mixed martial artists and what they went through daily. It wasn't pretty. They spent a lot of time on the ground practising submission moves and dangerous holds. Being my size, I'd be afraid of crushing somebody. I kept that idea in my head and went online to search for different martial arts gyms.

Wrestling was off limits for me. I felt uncomfortable getting on top of someone or letting someone get on top of me. Same with Judo. There were a few local places that taught Judo, but I didn't like the idea of being flipped or flipping someone else. Donny did Judo when we were kids. He made it pretty far and then quit to pursue guitar lessons. I eventually came across a cool place called King's Kickboxing, and it was located in the North End of Halifax so it couldn't have been too far from my neighbourhood. Kickboxing seemed really cool. The ad looked pretty badass: it had a caged fence in the background and giant gold font that said, "Stay Ready & In Shape." I was super nervous when I thought about joining, though. What would my mom think? I still hadn't come up with a plausible excuse I could use about my eye. *I tripped while walking to the bus? I fell in the weight room in gym class?*

I ignored all that for a moment, grabbed my phone, and called King's Kickboxing.

As it rang, my anxiety began to build.

"King's Kickboxing. This is Ryan speaking."

"Hi, Ryan. My name's Adrian, and I saw your ad online. I was wondering if I could do a trial class?"

"Yes, of course," he replied from his end. "What's your name?"

"My name is Adrian Carter," I answered.

"For sure, Adrian. Are you free this evening?"

"As in this evening, this evening? Wow. That's like, really soon."

"Yeah. This evening is this evening," Ryan said sarcastically.

"Ummm, sure. I'll be there. What time?"

"Be here at four-fifteen. Wear shorts and a t-shirt."

"Cool. I will."

"See you tonight, Adrian," Ryan said before he hung up the phone.

As I put my phone down, I realized it was 3:30 p.m. and I heard my front door open. It must have been my mom. I didn't know what to do and I began freaking out. What if she saw my eye? I shut my door to think of a plan.

"Adrian, are you home?" Mom called upstairs.

"Uhhh...Yeah. I'm actually just leaving, though," I called back as I grabbed shorts and a t-shirt from my dresser.

"Where to?" she asked as I came down the stairs moving in an odd direction so she couldn't see my whole face.

"To my kickboxing class," I told her with a smile.

"Kickboxing!? Adrian —"

I was out the door before she could finish the sentence. I knew my mom wouldn't like the idea of me joining kickboxing, but at least I told her the truth.

I found King's without any trouble. It was on Richards Street, but it was in the basement of a building just off the corner. As I walked down the flight of stairs toward the entrance, I could hear the sounds of fists hitting pads and people yelling as they did it. It sounded like adrenalin was rushing through a lot of people's blood.

I noticed everyone was wearing black shirts with KING'S written in gold on the front of them. A lean, bald, black man had seen me enter and he walked right up to me.

"Hello, I'm Ryan. I'm the head instructor here." He extended a hand. I shook it.

"Hi. I'm Adrian. We spoke on the phone earlier."

"Yep, that was me. Glad to see you could make it. Welcome to King's."

I could smell the sweat and feel the humidity coming toward me all at once. It felt overwhelming, and I was unsure if I even wanted to continue.

"All right, everyone. That ends class for today," Ryan called to the class. "Hit the showers."

I tended to avoid locker rooms, so I got changed in the washroom. I wore a white t-shirt and blue basketball shorts. When I came back out, Ryan was already on the mats waiting for me. I walked over and saw a pair of fingerless gloves on the floor.

"Those are yours for the night. Try them on," he said.

I did. It felt cool wearing fingerless gloves like the fighters did on TV.

"All right, big guy," he said. I hated being called that. "When I say left, punch left, when I say right, punch right."

"Okay," I replied. I began to get nervous.

"Left!"

I punched left.

"Right!"

I punched right.

We did that for about ten minutes, and I realized that I was really starting to sweat.

"All right," Ryan called out. "Now let's throw some kicks."

I didn't know how to throw kicks, so I did my best.

"Left kick!" he yelled.

I kicked awkwardly to the left.

"Right kick!" he yelled before my foot came back down. I kicked right as quickly as I could.

My kicks were pretty awful. I wasn't kicking like the people on TV, I was just lifting my legs toward the pads really fast, but it was actually pretty fun. I didn't want to stop. We continued this for about fifteen more minutes until I visibly slowed down, then Ryan lowered the pads.

"All right," he said. "I think that's enough for today."

I was covered in sweat and out of breath from the workout. I couldn't have kept going even if I wanted to.

"So, did you enjoy it?" he asked as we walked toward his desk.

"I loved it. It was a lot of fun," I replied, trying to hide my smile. I didn't want to look too keen, especially on my first night.

"Would you be interested in signing up for a month of classes?"

"Yes," I said with no hesitation. It was at that moment I knew I wanted to be there, even though I should have thought about it more first.

"Cool," he replied. "It's forty dollars a month. We have classes three times a week on Mondays, Wednesdays, and Fridays. We're open most of the day for hitting mats and such, but starting this week, classes that focus on technique begin at seven in the evening. Do you have any specific goals here?"

"Yeah," I told him. "I'm actually here to lose weight." I was a bit nervous putting those cards on the table. Telling someone that you're trying to lose weight is basically acknowledging the elephant in the room. I was fat, I knew

I was fat, and I was embarrassed about it.

"We'll make it happen," Ryan said confidently.

That made me smile.

"This is the new guy you told me about?" a voice asked from behind me. I turned around, startled, and saw a taller black woman who was a few years younger than Ryan with long, natural hair wearing the King's Kickboxing uniform.

"Yep. This would be him," Ryan said. "Adrian, meet Scarlett. For newcomers, we like to pair them up with folks who have been here for some time. Scarlett has been here for about three years."

"Wow," I said. "That's almost like all of high school."

"Yeah. Linear time, right?" Scarlett smiled at me. "I guess we're partners, big guy."

"Uh . . . yeah," I replied. I still didn't like being called that.

"Anyways, see you next class?" she asked. "You're gonna stick around, right?"

"Yeah, I think so."

"Since you're a student, I assume, I'll cut you a deal of seventy dollars for three months." Ryan smiled.

That was a great deal, but I didn't have seventy dollars. But maybe I could make seventy dollars fast. I didn't quite know how, but my parents had a lot of interesting things in our basement, things I knew they wouldn't miss, and things I knew I could make a quick buck off of.

"I'll have it to you next class," I told Ryan with way too much confidence.

"For sure." Ryan nodded. "See you soon, Adrian."

When I got home that night I managed to avoid my

parents and made it to my bedroom without them seeing my bruised face. I was big but sneaky. When I sat down on my bed, the question came to my mind: *how am I going to make seventy dollars?* I went to check my savings account (which was just a shoebox behind a bookshelf) and opened it up. I had thirty dollars in there. Two ten-dollar bills and a bunch of loonies and toonies.

I remembered my plan to check the basement.

I headed downstairs and searched around, hoping to find an artefact worth more than my parents' house. But honestly, all I found were dirty clothes I hadn't put in the wash and overdue library books from junior high. Nobody would pay much for those. I took one last look in a junk drawer and found some old gems. It was a box of records. I didn't even think my parents owned a record player. Inside the box there was a huge variety of blues, jazz, and what looked like metal. I thought my parents had mainly been into R&B. Me? I was all about hip-hop. But I couldn't picture either of them jamming out to metal or getting down with the blues. I thought maybe they wouldn't need them.

I grabbed my phone, took a few pictures of the box, and posted it to a group where people bought used items. I wrote, "Selling old records for $40. Barely used." That last part was probably a lie.

I put my phone down, and a few seconds later I heard the ringing sounds of notifications. I checked, and someone named Mel Woods kept commenting on the photos. The comments read:

Yooo! I've been looking for some records to play. I'm interested!
Sell me them!
I really need them!

*That was fast.* I went to Mel's profile and sent her a message.

**Me:** Hey. I'm following up about the records you wanted to buy.
**Mel Woods:** Yes! I want them all!
**Me:** Yeah, for sure. So are you located in the North End?
**Mel Woods:** Yep! Right by Queen Avenue. Can we meet at Redemption House Café tomorrow afternoon?
**Me:** Yeah that works. How does 1pm sound?
**Mel Woods:** Perfect ☺ See you then!

I put down my phone and carried the box of records to my room. It was a lot heavier than expected, but knowing I could sell those records and get a membership to King's made me feel better. Maybe everything would be fine. I'd join kickboxing, lose weight, and be ready to fight if Lewis ever approached me again.

# CHAPTER 2
## Mel

I woke up the next morning when my phone buzzed. It was a text from Donny.

**Donny:** Suspended for two weeks, grounded for four

My heart raced, and not in a good way. Donny had never been suspended before, and his parents must have been livid. It was my fault. I shouldn't have thrown the sandwich at Lewis. I should have just kept my mouth shut.

**Me:** Oh no. Donny, I'm so sorry. I shouldn't have gotten you involved.

**Donny:** You didn't bro. I chose to. Lewis is suspended for three weeks. I guess the security thought it was just a fight between me and him. They didn't see you get hit.

I wondered why nobody had called my house to tell my parents about it. I wasn't about to tell them. I was honestly more surprised Donny wasn't suspended for longer. The school was no nonsense when it came to fighting. He was a first offender though, which probably meant they had cut him some slack.

**Me:** Bro, whatever you need. I'm here for you, seriously
**Donny:** Thanks, but my mom is taking my phone away tomorrow, and I'm not really allowed to hang out with friends until I'm 'disciplined'
**Me:** That's rough bro. I wish it didn't go down like this
**Donny:** Me neither, but I wouldn't change how I reacted. Hear from you soon A.C.
**Me:** You know I hate being called that. Take care bro.

I wished I could have stood up for myself so Donny didn't have to. I was full of guilt, but I thought maybe learning kickboxing would prepare me for next time Lewis tried to bully me. When I went to the bathroom to look in the mirror, I saw that the bruise on my face had turned into a black eye.

"Shit," I said while looking at my reflection in the mirror. It wasn't a good look. My parents still hadn't really seen my eye since Lewis punched me. I didn't know how to cover it up with makeup or anything like that. While I was trying to think of a plan, there was a knock at the bathroom door.

"Adrian, hurry up in there." It was my mom's voice.

"Oh, shit," I said again. I couldn't let her see my eye.

"Watch your tongue," she replied.

I grabbed a wet cloth and pressed it against my face as if I was just washing up. I opened the door and darted straight to my bedroom.

Mom immediately started in about kickboxing and that she didn't like how violent it was, but I cut her off.

"I really liked the class, Mom. It was awesome and I'm going back." I continued walking away from her without making direct eye contact.

"But Adrian —" I shut my door before she could finish her sentence. All I heard was a loud sigh from the other side. I picked up the box without realizing how awkward it was to carry. My best bet to get to Redemption House was to take the bus that dropped me off a few blocks away.

I thought it'd be easy enough until I got to my bus stop. It was way too hot, and I didn't know why I decided to wear a black hoodie and jeans while carrying an awkward, flimsy box that I had to carry with both hands. I was already sweaty and gross. Everyone on the bus was looking at me. It was horrible. I could feel their eyes linger on me longer than they should have. I hated being the centre of anyone's attention, so a ten-minute bus ride felt like an eternity. I was relieved to press the stop button and get off.

Once I made it to Redemption House, I walked the box to the front steps of the café and sat down. I felt weird about meeting up with someone I had only met on the Internet. I didn't know who she was. What if she was just a troll trying to ghost me? It was even weirder thinking that was how some people dated. What if you thought someone was super cool and then you met them in person, and they ended up being totally different? I guess those were the risks people had to take.

I sat there for a few minutes before I heard someone yell, "Hey, dude!"

I looked across the parking lot and saw a girl around my age. Without being cliché — yes, my eyes widened and I could feel my chest tighten. Everything else just kind of disappeared. I saw Mel. She had beautiful deep, dark brown skin and long hair in a ponytail with bangs that came over her forehead. She wore a black button-up shirt that had five skeletons playing the keytar on it. It was super edgy looking.

"Hey," I managed to say. "You're Mel, right?"

"Yeah. I kind of look like my display photo, don't I?" she said sarcastically.

"Yeah," I replied. Truth be told, I'd been more focused on selling the records and I hadn't really looked through her profile.

"So . . . these are the records?" She pointed to the box sitting beside me.

"Uhh . . . yeah!" I told her as I came back to Earth. "They're here. They're barely used, I think."

"Oh, shit," she replied. "I didn't realize that it might be heavy. My dad was supposed to drive me back to our place, but he got called into work and couldn't."

"I could carry them back to your place," I volunteered.

"You don't have to, that's a pretty lame cliché," she said.

"Umm . . . yeah, you're right." I wished I could stop stammering.

"But, if you're going in the same direction, come along," she invited.

She seemed welcoming.

Mel picked up the box and we began walking back to her place. It was still really warm out. I was beginning to worry whether my sweat was causing me to smell bad, so I kept trying to sniff myself without her seeing me. I was an anxious ball of awkwardness and kept overthinking the possibilities of making myself look weird.

"It's really not too far from here," Mel said.

"Good to know. How much further?"

"Two blocks. Queens Avenue is pretty easy to miss if you drive by."

"Never been there before. Do you go to school around here?"

"Um . . . yeah. I know you from school, dude."

"Wait, what?" I said, confused. "You go to the same school as me?"

"Yeah. I see you sitting in the cafeteria alone a lot of the time."

She wasn't wrong. I mean, I usually hung out with Donny, but sometimes he got busy with his music club during the lunch hour so he left me alone. I was bad at making new friends, so being alone felt okay, even if it wasn't ideal.

"Yeah . . ." I said, worried. I was scared that she thought I was a loser.

"I saw what happened yesterday, too. That's the reason you have the shiner, I assume." She pointed at my eye.

"Yeah. That's the reason." I shrugged.

"Lewis is a douche."

"I would have never guessed."

"I'm sorry."

"Don't be," I mumbled.

Wow. She had seen everything. That's the most embarrassing part of being bullied publicly. Everyone sees it. Everyone knew what had happened and there was nothing I could do about it. I looked weak in front of everyone and Mel had seen it all. The only thing I could do to chase off the embarrassment was to change topics, so I asked, "How come I've never seen you at school before?"

"That's a good one." She sighed. "A lot of kids don't see me. Some of it is because I try to disappear, most of it is because I'm in the elite class. That means I'm stuck in front of a textbook or in a classroom most of the day."

*Oh gosh.* I had finally met someone who was in the elite class. It was kind of hard not to change my perspective of Mel after she told me that. For the most part, the elite class was full of pretentious jocks, classist students who thought they were better than everyone.

"Then there's me," Mel said, "Right in there with the pretentious jocks, the classist a-holes. There I am. The token brown girl who has to work twice as hard as everyone else just so people think I'm more than just a sprinkle of diversity."

Being the token sucks, and I could relate to that a lot of the time, especially in history class when teachers would ask me about the black perspective of Canadian history in front of an all-white class. It made me stick out more than I liked to.

"I can't believe you're wearing a black hoodie, man. It's so hot today," Mel observed.

Black was the only colour I felt comfortable wearing. Everything else turned see-through when I began to sweat, and I didn't like feeling exposed. But it *was* pretty hot, and I saw a bench nearby.

"Can we take a break?" I asked, feeling embarrassed.

"Yeah, sure. You tired?"

"The heat's getting to me."

We sat down, and I began taking breaths. I was so out of shape and hated having to do that. Mel probably thought I was weird and gross, but she sat there with me.

"So . . . that's really shitty that Lewis told the entire cafeteria how much you weighed," Mel mentioned as she picked up the box.

"I know," I replied. "That's why I'm selling all this stuff. I'm trying to lose weight."

"Oh yeah?" she asked in an excited voice. "How are you going to lose weight?"

"I'm joining a kickboxing gym."

"That's . . . pretty sick," Mel told me.

"Thanks?" I laughed.

"No, for real. That takes guts, dude. Losing weight is hard. I know this because I'm focusing my studies on healthy eating and living. If you need help with anything, let me know, okay?"

"How can you help?" I was curious.

"Well, I know a lot about nutrition and a lot of good exercises to help strengthen muscles. I'm also a black belt in Karate."

"I mean . . . I think that would be pretty cool." I would have never guessed that Mel was a black belt in Karate, but it sounded awesome and having someone who knew what they were doing would be a major help. And I guess it would be cool to spend time with Mel.

"Cool. I'll give you my number once we get to my place — which is behind this bench." She giggled. "C'mon!"

I turned around and saw a street sign that read Queen's Avenue. I frowned and followed her. She sat down on the front steps of her house, took out a notebook from her jeans pocket, ripped out a page, and wrote down her number.

"Here ya go, Adrian." She smiled. "Also, before I forget." She reached back into her pocket and gave me two twenty-dollar bills.

"Thanks for the records, man. When you posted the picture, I saw some goldies I've been trying to get my hands on for a while."

"No problem. I'm just happy they're going somewhere where they'll be played properly."

"Awesome. Come over for a chill session sometime?"

There was no way I would refuse that.

"Yes! Of course," I told her.

"Well, you have my number. Don't act like you don't." She stuck her tongue out at me. "See you soon." She grabbed the records and went inside.

I was forty dollars richer and had a beautiful girl's phone number. I felt a lot better than I had yesterday. I stuck her number in my wallet and made my way home.

Having Mel on my mind completely erased the memory of my black eye, so when I walked inside my house my mom's sudden screech startled me.

"Adrian, what the hell happened to you?" I froze.

"Oh. This?" I pointed to my eye.

"Yes. That," Mom said, unimpressed with me trying to play stupid.

I didn't know what to say. I couldn't tell her about Lewis. That would make it worse. She would show up at my school, talk to the principal, Lewis would get in more trouble, and of course everyone would find out it was because of me and I'd be called a snitch. So, I lied.

"Oh . . . it happened at kickboxing last night. It was an accident."

"Wait, Adrian. I don't understand. Why kickboxing? Why now?"

I didn't really want to tell my mom that I was trying to lose weight. It was embarrassing. I just wanted to do take the class, but I knew she wouldn't let it go unless I was honest, so that's when I decided to just tell her the truth.

"I'm trying to lose weight," I sighed.

I was never open with my parents about my weight. I know they wanted me to get in shape, but never outwardly told me so. It was their open secret. I could tell by some subtle signs it was what they wanted. They would sometimes ask if I wanted to start drinking protein shakes or if I wanted to start jogging or eat healthier. So when I told my mom the truth, her body language changed. It went from being concerned and frustrated to sympathetic.

"Oh. You should have said so. But kickboxing, really?"

"Yeah. I mean, I've always wanted to do a martial art. It's a pretty intense workout, too."

"I'm not here to police you, Adrian. You're going to be

a grown man soon. The decisions you make are yours, but I'm not too fond of this idea. Do it if you like it, but be more careful," she told me.

"I will," I replied as I made my way to my bedroom.

It had felt really awkward to open up to my mom about my weight, but it couldn't have gone any smoother than that. I had most of what I needed. I had the money to pay for a few months of kickboxing classes. Now it was time to see if I could really keep up.

# CHAPTER 3
# New Life

I didn't realize how much it would hurt. My legs felt like
noodles so I laid down on the mats at King's as I heard
Ryan yell, "Thirty more seconds until break is over!"

Scarlett stood over me with a humorous grin. "Feeling
down, big guy?"

"Everything hurts," I moaned.

"It will. But over time your body will adjust to it."

I hoped that was true. I felt so out of breath. Everyone
else seemed to be keeping up with the class, and then
there was me. I could attribute it to being the new guy,
or I could be honest and say it was because I was out of
shape.

"Here, let me help you up." Scarlett reached for my hand.

I was afraid I might be too heavy for her.

"I don't think that's a good idea," I tried to say, but she

grabbed my hand and pulled me up in one swift motion. She was strong.

"All right, dude. We're going back to kicking drills," she explained. "Go back to the wall and kick forward until you get to the other end of the gym."

It sounded easy enough.

It wasn't easy. My legs were very heavy, and my entire body was sore.

"Keep going, Adrian!" I could hear Scarlett yell. "Go! Go! Go!"

Having support in my corner helped. I thought it would be enough to keep me going, but sometimes your body can override that and decide to shut down. Kind of like mine did.

I was on the floor, inhaling through my mouth. I couldn't breathe very well, so I took big breaths and closed my eyes. When I opened them again, I could see both Ryan and Scarlett kneeling over me with a ton of other faces from the class behind them.

"You all right, big man?" Ryan asked. "You went down pretty hard."

"I'm fine." I tried to get back up.

"No, you're not," Scarlett said as she put her hand on my chest, holding me in place. "Stay down for a second. You're going to get light-headed if you get back up."

"I'm good," I tried to explain. I didn't want to look weak in front of everyone. I had to show them all that I could keep up like they did, even if I was bigger.

"Stay down," Ryan said sternly. "Scarlett, can you take the kid home?"

"Yep. Give him five and send him my way."

Ryan passed me a bottle of water and I guzzled down every last drop of it.

A few minutes later he helped me up, patted me on the back, and said, "See you next class, kid. This stuff happens, don't sweat it."

I went to the washroom, changed my clothes and grabbed my gear. I met Scarlett in the parking lot. She honked her horn at me and I got in her car.

"It happens. Don't worry about it," she reassured me.

"It's just so embarrassing to pass out in front of everyone."

"I know. But trust me, it could be worse. After my first class at King's, I threw up right in this parking lot. In front of everyone," she confessed.

Vomiting in front of a group of people might be a tad more embarrassing than fainting.

"Okay. That actually makes me feel a bit better."

"See? This stuff happens to everyone. Just take it easy. Where do you live, kid?"

"I live on Maple Street. Right off the corner."

"Cool. That's not too far from here."

By the time we got to my place the sun had already set and moonlight splashed onto my driveway. My house was three levels high, and my room was just above the garage where Scarlett parked.

"Again, take it easy, okay? You don't want to overstress your body. Let it rest, eat some food, and drink some water when you get inside," Scarlett suggested.

"Will do. Thank you," I told her as I closed her car door.

When I got inside, I didn't eat or drink anything. I went straight to my bedroom and collapsed on my bed. My body was in pain, so I laid in my bed and watched the moonlight make its way through my curtains and onto my face. I looked at the stars. They were few and far between, but they still put me at ease. I thought about Mel. I wanted to give her a call and ask about healthy foods to eat. I had been eating a lot of crap — cookies, chips, and burgers. That had probably contributed to my lacklustre performance in class.

I sat up and looked over at my desk. On it laid Mel's phone number. It'd been about a week since I sold her those records. I'd thought about calling her, but I didn't want to seem clingy. But something about the sky made me feel like everything would be all right, so I decided to grab her number and dial it. I thought, *What's the worst that could happen?*

She picked up. "Hello?"

"Hey. It's Adrian," I greeted her.

"Dang, dude. A girl gives you her number and you wait almost a week to call her back? That's edgy."

*Whoa.* I wasn't expecting a reply like that. Anxiety clawed its way inside of my chest. I should have called her earlier.

"I'm sorry," I told her.

"Ha, don't be. I'm only messing with you. So, what has you calling Mel Woods tonight?"

I didn't want to say I was lonely, even though I was. But I also had a reason to call her.

"Yeah . . . I kinda wanted to talk to you about, like, healthy foods and stuff to eat."

"Oh, yeah? That's kind of my specialty as of late. How can I help you?"

"Uh . . . so, yeah, I'm just trying to find ways to lose weight and replace the junk food I already eat with something else," I explained.

"All right. Just so you know, your diet isn't going to completely change overnight. It takes time. For weight loss, I'd say try going low carb. Eat lots of chicken. Cut out bread, chips, french fries, basically everything that tastes amazing. Throw it all out the window."

I didn't want to throw everything that tasted amazing out of the window, though I knew it was necessary. I picked up a piece of paper and started writing things down.

We spoke for a while, and she gave me the rundown on stuff to avoid, but also told me to let my body adjust to change. It wouldn't happen overnight. Her voice was lovely, but it also left a lot up to my imagination.

"So, yeah. Eventually, the goal is to just stop eating shit I guess," she finished.

"That sounds like a good goal," I replied.

"Yeah, harder than it seems, though. Hey, your records are pretty rad by the way. I've been trying to use my mom's old record player for something. I really dig the album by Iron Beards, and the music pisses my dad off, which is a bonus."

"You like pissing off your dad?"

"Not really. But he doesn't say anything when I play it. I just hear a loud sigh upstairs every hour or so. He passed this thing down to me, so he made his own choice."

I laughed. It was a funny way to look at it. I wondered what her father was like. Was he a hard-ass or super chill? By the sound of it, it seemed as if there could have been a bump in the road between her and her father, so I asked.

"What's your dad like?"

"An art snob. He's a classical guy, owns a music shop I work at. It's called Woods Classical Music. Stupid, right? I know. It's like he only listens to music by dead white guys from the 1800s. Meanwhile I'm into heavy metal and punk rock. I love concerts and a good mosh pit."

*What the hell is a mosh pit?* I thought.

I dared to ask the most important question. "So . . . do you want to hang out or something, sometime soon?"

"I feel like I could arrange that. When were you thinking?" I could hear her smile from the other end of the line.

I smiled, too.

"Umm . . . you know. Whenever, I guess."

"How about this weekend? We can have a workout day or something and chill afterward if you're down."

"Yeah, I'd be so down for that." I sounded way too excited.

"Awesome. Meet me Sunday at my place? One o'clock?"

"That works."

"Cool. Wear shorts and a t-shirt this time. It's going to be hot. Talk to you soon, weird boy."

I didn't know what made me weird, and I didn't know what to say to that other than, "Okay. See you then."

She hung up the phone.

I looked over the notes I had taken from Mel, and they started out pretty basic:

- No carbs
- Lots of chicken

- Don't eat after 8pm
- Eat until you're not hungry anymore, not until you're full

Beyond that was just doodles of her and me. My imagination got the better of me sometimes.

I tossed my notebook at my desk, put Mel's number back in my wallet and looked at the sky a bit longer, wishing that the moonlight could wash away the pain I was feeling. *Maybe someday I'll be skinny*, I thought. *Maybe Mel will like me if I am.*

# CHAPTER 4

# More Than a Number

That Sunday morning, I stepped on the scale. After a week of kickboxing classes, I was surprised to see that I was down only three pounds. I weighed 277 pounds. As far as progress goes, I was disappointed. I was tired of being fat. I just wanted to have a body I felt good in. I wanted a body that didn't need to wear a 5XL t-shirt. I wanted a body I could wear shirtless to the beach. I wanted a body that I could do a cartwheel in. It was something that I was working toward, but it was something I didn't have, so disappointment still filled me to the brim.

Mel had mentioned doing some exercises with me that afternoon. I was really nervous about it, though. More often than not, I was awkward when it came to talking to girls, so I hoped I wouldn't say anything weird or make her think I was any weirder. The "weird boy" comment had stuck with me. I put on basketball shorts and a large black t-shirt so that if I sweated a lot, it wouldn't be see-through.

When I got to Mel's place I found her sitting on her steps.

"Hey, weird boy," she greeted.

I frowned.

"You're frowning already? It's all downhill from here, buddy." Mel laughed. "Come on," she commanded as she started walking. I followed her.

"So, uh . . . what are we doing today?" I asked.

"A bunch of stuff. I want to focus on your core, though."

"And that requires . . . what?"

"Doing what I tell you to do."

"You like bossing people around, don't you?" I said.

"I like giving guidance. Sometimes that requires me to be a bit of a hard-ass. But don't worry, you'll thank me someday."

We walked to a big open field by her place. There were some dogs running around and a few people having picnics. It was a very open area that had enough space for everyone, but that was what made me nervous.

"Uh . . . so we're going to do this in public?" I asked.

"Yep. I suppose so. We don't have gym memberships, and it's gorgeous out here. Where's a better place to do it?"

"Somewhere where people won't stare at the fat kid trying to exercise."

"You're shy," she realized. "But listen, if people make fun of someone who is overweight and trying to change that, then they're assholes. I got your back. Don't be afraid to fall back every once in a while."

I took her word for it. I hated being so vulnerable out in the open, but I didn't want to go back and we were already there. I didn't want to let Mel down, and I didn't want to let myself down, either.

I sat down on the grass and watched Mel do some stretching. I admired the passion she put into herself. Though it got uncomfortable when she looked me in the eye.

"Stop staring at me and start stretching, weird boy."

She'd called me "weird boy" twice within twenty minutes. That wasn't good. I shouldn't have stared. It was a bad look. I extended my legs forward and leaned against them as far as I could, then stretched my arms one at a time.

"All right, we're going to do some planks," she instructed.

"Like, lying on top of weird things like cars and sidewalks?" I said sarcastically.

"Funny." She wasn't impressed. "You know what a plank is, right?"

"I do. I hate them," I sighed.

"Then don't wait for me." She grinned.

I let out another sigh and got into position. A plank is when you have your body straight and lift your stomach off the ground. Both arms rest by your head to hold you up, and your feet stick beside each other so they keep you in position. Then you have to hold yourself up without letting your stomach touch the ground or having your butt too far in the air.

"Let's go!" Mel cheered.

I lifted. It hurt, and it was a difficult position to hold. But change wouldn't come without sacrifice.

I held the position as long as I could, but my face began

turning red and my stomach felt like it was going to submit to gravity, so I tried to stealthily lift my butt, and when I did I could feel Mel's foot press against it, sending it back down.

"Not so fast." She grinned as she lowered my butt back into position. "You try to look at mine and I'll put yours back in its place."

*Well played*, I thought. I was in too much pain to say it out loud. I lasted for about five more seconds and fell to the ground.

"That all you got?" She kneeled down beside me.

"That's all the love I got for planking." I tried to catch my breath.

"Then we'll move on to something else," she said as she patted my head with her hand.

We moved on to a lot of things. We did sit-ups, push-ups, and three awful sets of leg lifts.

As I was finishing up the lifts, Mel was counting them with me.

"Come on, Adrian! You're at twenty-six, twenty-seven, twenty-eight."

I let out a cry and stayed down. It hurt too much, my body couldn't do it, everything burned beneath my skin, and I didn't want to keep going.

"Come on, Adrian. You got this."

"I can't," I whined. I didn't want to let Mel down, but my body wouldn't go any further. It was way too hard, so I bit my lip and gave up.

I leaned back into the grass, putting my hands on my head. *Working your core hurts.* I had been letting myself down for too long. My body was like a punching bag, but instead of years of physically hitting it, I just binge ate. From fast food to always asking for seconds and thirds, I ate a lot, and I ate too much, so navigating through simple tasks was hard enough. Every time I overate, I weighed down a part of myself.

"That's all right, Adrian. You tried." She kneeled down and gave me a gentle "good job" punch on my arm.

"Let's get you some water," she said.

She helped me get to my feet, and when we stood up, I could hear giggling from a distance. I turned to see, and there were two boys in the grass, pointing at me while laughing. One of them was wearing a sleeveless tank top and had a mohawk, the other was shirtless and had hard abs. They weren't too much older than us.

"What's so funny?" Mel asked.

"Don't." I tried to stop her.

"What is it?" she asked again, ignoring me.

"You're helping a lost cause. He's just going to get diabetes anyways," one of them yelled and then laughed.

I looked away. I didn't have the energy to hide my hurt.

"Yeah, and you'll end up getting my fist in your face," she yelled back.

"Oh, wow, you're so badass," one of them said.

"Try me, douchebags." She gave them a death glare and silence filled the air.

"Whatever," the shirtless guy said as they both got up and walked away. Mel looked back and saw I had turned away. I didn't want her to see me upset. That's what hurt the most, being labelled a lost cause. I had made so many mistakes with my body, and I wanted to begin making some good choices. But being labelled a lost cause was not only hurtful, it scared me. Maybe I wouldn't lose the weight. Maybe I would keep being obese and die at a young age. Maybe I'd never be able to fit into anything under a 5XL or take my shirt off at a beach. Maybe this was it. That's what scared me the most.

"I'm sorry, Adrian," Mel said in a soft voice. She put a hand on my shoulder and turned my face toward her. I felt a tear rolling down my cheek.

"It's okay to cry, y'know. I know you boys don't like doing that much, but you don't have to hide your feelings here. You can be you. And forget those losers, man. Focus on you and me. We're going to get through this together, I promise."

I appreciated those words more than I could tell her. They sunk into me and made me feel as if someone genuinely cared. That was something I lacked. I never had many friends. I would never cry in front of Donny; I would never cry in front of my parents. I was always full of so much fear, so much sadness, regret, and shame when I looked at my body. I was just a reminder of all my failures. But it was also the only thing that was truly mine. My body made me feel like I was hopelessly lost at sea. Then there was Mel — she was like a light bringing me closer to the shore, creating a calm to my storm.

"Let's just get out of here," I said, walking away. She walked with me and held my hand along the way.

We headed back to Mel's place, and she asked, "Wanna come in? I wanna make sure you're okay, man."

It was a nice offer, but after what had happened, I just needed to be alone.

"Not today, Mel. I kind of just want to go home." I felt really embarrassed and very fragile.

"I understand," she replied. "I'm sorry if that was weird. If you need someone to vent to, then just text me, all right?"

"All right," I replied. "Thanks for today, by the way."

"That's what I'm here for," she reassured me.

I cracked a smile and made my way home.

When I got there, I went straight to my bathroom. I took off all of my clothes and stepped onto the scale again. It said 278.9 pounds

"What the hell," I whispered to myself. I was annoyed. I didn't understand why I gained weight after a workout like that. It upset me because it made me realize how far away my goal was. *How much pain do I have to go through to make the numbers on the scale go down?* It was a question I didn't know the answer to.

The next few days, after every workout and meal, I would step on the scale only to be furious at the numbers not going down. It was always so disappointing to see. I couldn't stop thinking about those guys making fun of me at the park. If I got the weight off, then that wouldn't happen anymore. I would probably be a lot happier, too. I could probably fall in love, I would be able to take my shirt off at the beach, and be able to play sports. The opportunities that came with a healthy body seemed endless.

I also thought about Mel. I wondered if she thought I was gross. I thought she was beautiful. She was very no-nonsense, but also made time for me and let me be honest about my insecurities. That was what I liked about her. The next few days, she helped get my butt in position with planking, and I could feel myself being able to stay in position longer each time. Everything felt a bit easier as my body began getting used to it.

"All right, weird boy," Mel said. "Twenty-six, twenty-seven, twenty-eight." She counted my leg lifts again. We were in the same spot as before. She had convinced me to come back to that spot, and said if anyone messed with me she would give them an ass kicking.

"Twenty-nine!" she yelled.

That was the furthest I had made it into the leg lifts. My body was in so much pain, but I still had fight in me. I could feel my muscle building itself up, and I took a deep breath and gave my legs one last lift to thirty. Mel jumped with joy and landed right on the grass to hug me.

"You did it!"

"Yeah," I gasped trying to ignore the pain in my legs. "I friggin' did it."

"Wanna get up?" she asked.

"Not yet. I just wanna chill."

We both laid in the grass and looked at the clouds. We joked, giggled, and gazed at the sky for a while.

"You should get some food," she suggested. "I can cook you up something if you want to come over."

"No. I'm okay," I told her. "I, uh . . . I have to go home and do some stuff."

"Like what?"

"I'm gonna go home and weigh myself."

"Are you dumb?"

*Dumb? Why would I be dumb for wanting to weigh myself?*

"I want to see my progress," I explained.

"No, dude. You weigh yourself in the morning. Not in the middle of the day. Throughout the day your weight fluctuates, and it'll just make you upset."

That explained a lot.

"Oh," I said.

"Oh?" Mel replied. "How often do you weigh yourself?"

"Like . . . three times a day."

"Dude." She shook her head. "No. Stop doing that."

"Why? I just want to track it."

"You're only supposed to weigh yourself like once every two weeks, otherwise you'll just get frustrated."

It made sense. If my weight was going up and down during the day then it was pointless to keep weighing myself so excessively. I just hadn't known about that before.

"Oh," I said again. I felt stupid but didn't want to admit it. "I should stop doing that."

Mel shook her head at me. "Duh. Anyways, you wanna come over later? I should probably take a shower and you should, too." She pointed at my sweaty armpits.

"Yeah, I'll be over later," I told her.

I got to my feet and she stuck her tongue out at me. I stuck mine out at her as well and we both laughed.

# CHAPTER 5
# Shine

I stood outside of Mel's house that evening and knocked on the door. To my surprise, it wasn't her who answered the door, but an older white man.

"Can I help you?" he asked.

"Uh . . . yeah. I'm here to see Mel," I replied.

"Oh, Melody. My daughter."

*Melody?* Huh, that threw me off. I guessed that was what Mel was short for.

"Dad!" I heard from behind him. "Don't call me that. It's just Mel."

"All right, Mel." The man let out a gentle laugh as he opened the door wide enough for me to see Mel.

"Hi, Adrian." She was trying to hide her smile from her dad. "Come on. I'll show you around."

It was the first time I had stepped foot in Mel's house.

The place was a lot bigger than it looked on the outside. She hadn't been kidding when she said her dad was into classical art. There were paintings and sculptures placed all along the entrance hallway. At the end of it I could see a grandfather clock engraved with "WOODS." Each wall had a painting of some sort, ranging from, "This was made at least two hundred years before I was born," to "this was made fifty years before I was born."

"Ignore the paintings and follow me," Mel said as she grabbed my hand and pulled me along.

She took me down a flight of stairs that led to the basement. There were rock and roll posters all over the walls, a record player sitting at the end of the bed, and I could see the old box of records sitting on the floor outside of her closet.

"This is it." She spread her arms dramatically. "As you can see, there's a bit of contrast between my father's tastes and mine."

"That was your dad?" I asked, still a bit confused.

"Yes. He's my dad. And yes, he's my biological father."

"Oh," I said out loud. "It's just that, he's —"

"White and I'm brown? I know. My grandparents from my mom's side are from India, and my dad's side of the family? England. Why do you think my last name is Woods?

"Yeah, that makes sense."

"You're mixed, too. Isn't one of your parents white?"

"No. Both my parents are mixed," I explained. "They're both half black and half white. So I guess that makes me half black and half white."

"Two halves make a whole, right?" Mel laughed.

"Anyways, I was listening to the Iron Beards today. It pisses my dad off sometimes, but he's too shy to say anything," she told me as she pulled a record from the box. The album cover was awesome. It had five black men with beards that were made of iron. Music in the 80s was something else. Mel began playing the album and she cranked it really loud no doubt so her dad could hear. She leapt on her bed and started jumping up and down.

"Jump on my bed with me!" she shouted.

"Ummm . . ."

"Ummm . . . what!?" she asked, still hopping up and down.

"I don't want to break it."

"Pffttt." She jumped off the mattress and landed in front of me. "Then dance with me here," she said as she started moving back and forth with the music. Dancing was something I wasn't brave enough to do. I already felt awkward enough in my body as it was, but actually being able to move so fluidly and carelessly like Mel? I just couldn't.

"What? Are you scared?" she asked. "It's only me, dude. You have nothing to fear. Pretend we're in a mosh pit." She grabbed my hands and moved my arms back and forth while she was jumping up and down.

"What's a mosh pit?"

"I'll show you sometime."

She got me to twist and turn with her, and though dancing wasn't my thing, I was having fun.

"Why do you like to annoy your dad?" I tried speaking over the music while still moving my arms.

"Honestly, Adrian? My dad doesn't want me to be the person I am. He wants me to wear dresses instead of ripped jeans. He wants me to learn painting instead of going to concerts. I'm not the ideal daughter he wants, and I have to let him know that I'm never changing who I am."

It must have been difficult to have a parent who wanted you to be something that you didn't want to be. My parents were always okay with me acting how I pleased. But I suppose I wasn't so much out of the ordinary. They saw me as a good kid for the most part, with my heart in the right place.

Mel rocked her head back and forth, letting her hair go, and I could see her smile even when her hair covered her eyes. She was so beautiful. And there I was, an awkward fat guy, not even able to dance to a simple rhythm while she looked so fearless and free. She was someone I aspired to be.

"Why are you in the elite class?" I asked, trying to clumsily manoeuvre my feet.

"I only applied because my dad wants me to go to university after I graduate. But what if I don't want to go to university? What if I want to get a car and just drive across the country, travel, and head to rallies to be the social justice warrior he can't stand? Why can't I live life how I see fit? I can win a lot of battles against my dad, but I couldn't win that one," she vented. I had never thought about what I wanted to do after I graduated. I was still in grade ten, so I felt like those decisions were a long while away. Those decisions didn't have to be made anytime soon for Mel either, but pressure like that could build on someone.

Mel stopped the music and sat down on her bed, catching

her breath. "That wasn't so bad, was it?"

"No. I'm just glad no one saw me." I laughed. She laughed, too.

"So, tell me about Lewis. Want me to punch him in the face?"

"I wouldn't want you to get suspended. My friend Donny already did," I explained. "Lewis bullies me a lot. I hate him, and I hate how he made me look weak in front of everyone a couple weeks ago. Him and Donny have been suspended ever since," I vented.

"You're afraid of looking weak?" Mel asked.

"I mean, yeah. I want to be strong. I want be able to fight someone who messes with me."

"You are strong, just in a different way. You're gentle."

I didn't want to be gentle. I wanted to be the guy nobody messed with, and I was hoping kickboxing would help me get there.

"Bullies suck, dude. I'm sorry. He shouldn't be treating you like that, and next time I'll give him something to cry about," she said.

Suddenly Mel got up and asked, "Wanna go for a jog?"

I was still hesitant after what had happened in the park — getting used to one area was one thing, but jogging to a bunch of different places? I wasn't sure about that at all. Even though it was dark and there were fewer people outside, I didn't like anyone seeing me exercise. It felt humiliating. I chose not to say anything at first.

"You afraid of the dark, Adrian?" Mel persisted.

"No," I said defensively. "I just don't want people to see me jogging. I feel embarrassed."

"What's wrong with people seeing a dude trying to get in shape?"

"Nothing. Just . . . people don't always see you how you want them to see you," I sighed.

"I can relate. But we should go. I want to take you somewhere. I promise it'll be cool."

"If you promise." I grinned.

"Come on, weirdo," she replied.

I followed her into the night. Jogging in the dark was calming. Everything felt so fluid, like we were on autopilot. Mel made sure to jog at my pace so I could keep up. Our feet moved in sequence. She really cared about me, and I really cared about her, but I was too shy to say anything. I would have been lying if I said that I didn't have a crush on her, but I didn't know how to tell her. I was worried that she wouldn't feel the same way and it might become awkward. I was grateful for her friendship, and I didn't want to chance losing it.

"Over here!" Mel said, almost out of breath. We were getting close to our school. We jogged past the park and made our way up the path that led to the entrance.

"Taking night classes?" I joked.

"Funny." She still wasn't impressed with my humour. "Follow me."

We continued toward the school and walked past the entrance to an old fire exit.

She stopped. "I want to show you something up there."

"Up where?"

Mel took a few steps back, ran forward, and jumped high enough to grab hold of the ladder that was a few feet above our heads. She pulled herself up, climbed to the first level of the fire escape, and sent the ladder down.

"Up here." She waved at me. "Come on."

My eyes widened. I wasn't sure why I did it. I usually wouldn't do stuff like that, but I did it. I climbed the ladder and followed Mel.

She led me to the roof of the school. To my surprise, there was a garden that expanded all across the section where we stood.

"I take care of this place most of the time. I've never brought anyone up here. Especially boys. Consider yourself lucky," she told me as she sat down on the rooftop. "You can sit with me, dude. Don't be so nervous." I walked across the rooftop, gazing at a good chunk of the neighbourhood from a view I hadn't seen it from before. The trees, paths, and streetlights looked like a maze and I was able to watch it all as I sat down beside Mel.

"I'm up here a lot. The school lets me do it because I look after the garden. I'm not supposed to come up here at night time, but I do. That's when I have to take the fire escape," Mel explained.

"It's beautiful up here," I said as I examined my surroundings.

I looked up and saw a handful of stars.

"When I was younger, my parents used to take me camping by a lake where the stars reflected off the water. We used to skip rocks with the stars — that's what Mom used to say, anyways," Mel said.

"What happened to your mom?" I asked, without thinking.

Mel let out a deep breath. "My parents went through a really bad divorce. My mom . . . she moved halfway across the country, and I don't hear from her much. Last I heard, she has a new boyfriend. I found out my dad blocked her number on our family phone. I speak to her on my cell, but I haven't heard from her in a while."

"I'm sorry," I said. I really wasn't expecting that at all. Mel must have felt really lost because of it.

"Don't sweat it. He's a control freak. I have a lot of baggage. It's whatever."

She waved it off while grabbing a cigarette from her pocket. "Do you smoke?"

"Umm . . ."

"That means no. I'm not going to pressure you like this is some after-school special."

I laughed away the awkwardness and watched her light it up.

"So . . . your real name is Melody?" I asked.

Mel sighed. "Yeah. I don't really use my full name at all. It seems a bit pretentious."

"I think it's a beautiful name."

She gave me a glare, took a puff of her cigarette, and let me see her smile.

"I like your smile," I blurted. I didn't mean to, but then I blushed, and she blushed, too.

"I think I like yours, too," she admitted. "You're gentle, and I appreciate it."

I was glad someone appreciated me. I was especially glad it was Mel. I hadn't known her for long, but she was already so special to me. I wanted to tell her, but I was afraid to. What if it didn't work out? She might have been too punk rock, and maybe I was too hip-hop. But somewhere along the line, she made my heart dance like a rock she was skipping across the ocean. Mel made me break routine. I liked it because my life had always been set in stone for the most part. I would do the same things — go to school, get bullied, go home and cry, stress eat, gain more weight — it was a circle that led me nowhere. But then I met the hard-ass, confident, illuminating soul that was Melody. I wanted to tell her that I thought she was wonderful, and that I had a crush on her, and that she was the first girl to make me ever feel butterflies. Serious butterflies.

"Hey —" I began.

"Hey, what?" she interrupted. "If you're gonna say something, say it."

"I'm trying, okay?" I lowered my shoulders and took a breath.

That's when she realized I was serious and said, "All right," in a soft voice.

When you tell someone that you like them, there is always this awkward moment before and after you say anything, because you know something is coming, but you're just not quite sure how it's going to sound. I knew what I *wanted* to say. I wanted to tell Mel that I thought she was wonderful, and that I had a crush on her, and that she was someone I'd like to take to a dance or on a date. But words don't come so easy when you're terrified. So, a lot of the conversation was me reciting poetic masterpieces like: "Hey . . . I think you're pretty great." Or: "I'm, uhhh, pretty bad at this, but you, um, you're great." And the best one yet:

"So, I know we have different music tastes but you're still pretty great."

She frowned and asked, "Are you trying to tell me that you like me?"

Even though that was exactly what I'd been trying to say, answering was still not easy. But I took a shot in the dark. "Yeah. I like you . . . a lot . . . and stuff." I shied away from eye contact. Anxiety landed in my chest like a spiky lump. I was sure I had just ruined something great. *I shouldn't have said anything.* I shut my eyes and wished the roof of the school would open up and swallow me. Then I felt her hand underneath my chin. I opened my eyes as she turned my face toward her.

"Hey, sweet boy," she whispered. "I think you're pretty great, too." She pulled me gently forward and met me half-way. She pressed her lips against mine. My heart sped up, and I closed my eyes again. The lump of anxiety evaporated and was replaced with a warmth that felt like magic. I kissed Mel, and she kissed me back. Everything was perfect. I didn't care if she was punk rock and I was hip-hop. The only thing I wanted to hear was her melody. I could hear it loud and clear; I could hear her melody at the centre of my universe.

# CHAPTER 6
# Bad Habit

Mel told me that she didn't care how big I was. She said that she saw an honest heart and asked if I could make space in it for her. I said of course I could. It's weird when you fall for someone. When I kissed Mel on the rooftop that night, something inside of me thought that everything would be okay. Something inside of me let me love myself for the first time in a long time. But when I walked her home that night, and after we said our goodbyes, I may have left my heart open for too long. Worry had crept in when I got home. I looked at myself in the mirror and was disgusted. Then I took off my clothes and I stepped on the scale. It didn't help. It only made things more drastic. It said 275 pounds. I was losing weight, but not at the pace I wanted to. I was pissed off because of it. So I decided to take things into my own hands.

The next day I didn't eat anything. The only thing I allowed in my body was water. I was running on empty when Ryan made us do laps around the gym.

"Five more laps!" he yelled.

"Watch out!" I heard as Scarlett passed me.

She had passed me three times at that point, and I felt a bit embarrassed. I was taking small breaths so I wouldn't overwhelm my lungs. I was a bit surprised I had enough energy to run without food in my stomach, but that didn't stop my hunger. I just wanted to eat, but I had to sacrifice something.

I finished the laps like Ryan told us. After that, I went straight to the corner and grabbed my water bottle, guzzling down every last drop that was in there.

"All right, everyone," Ryan called again. "We're hitting the pads. Find a partner."

I wondered how much longer I could last. When your stomach is empty, everything else seems a lot heavier. Me being massively overweight didn't help that equation. Before I even turned around to find a teammate, I heard Scarlett say, "Howdy, partner," with a funny accent.

"Hi there." I took in a wave of air.

I liked Scarlett a lot. She was like the big sister I never had.

She grabbed a pair of boxing pads and stood firmly on the ground. I put on some boxing gloves and threw a right, left, right, left.

"Be creative," she said. "Try some jabs like Ryan showed you before."

I stood with my right hand forward and jabbed away. I could feel myself getting tired, but I kept going and going until I felt light-headed again. I had to fight through it. I couldn't faint twice. Ryan wouldn't want that — he'd ask me to take time off again. I powered through it until Ryan told us to switch. That's when I took a knee and told Scarlett that I needed a minute.

"All right," she said in a concerned tone. "You okay, kid?"

"Yeah. Just tired," I lied.

"You've been half-assing all class."

I'd hoped she wouldn't notice.

"You don't have any energy, do you?" she asked.

"Not really. No."

"What did you eat today?" She knelt down to my level.

"Just water."

"Water? Dude, you need to eat something before you come to class. I'm taking you home."

"No," I tried to argue. "I have to finish."

"No way, kid." She grabbed my hand and pulled me up. "You need food on the double."

I wasn't going to eat. I'd just end up eating the food and stepping on the scale and being disappointed because of it. I didn't know what exactly my plan was in the long term, but I needed to lose as much weight as I could.

"No, I'm okay." I leaned against the wall only to slide back down. I wasn't okay.

Scarlett took me to her car and dug in the glove compartment. She pulled out a protein bar. "Eat this," she demanded, shoving the bar into my hand.

As soon as I ripped open the wrapper I could smell the chocolate mixed with peanut butter, and devoured the entire bar.

"Get in, kid. I'm taking you home."

I did as she instructed and she hit the gas.

As Scarlett drove me home she got straight to the point. "What's your deal, kid? Why aren't you eating?"

I explained to her how often I weighed myself and how I wanted to lose weight to impress Mel.

"That's mega unhealthy," she told me. "Don't lose weight because you think it'll help you find love."

"She already likes me back," I said. "We kissed and everything."

"And everything?" She laughed. "You sound like you're a stud. Cut that shit out."

I wasn't a stud. I just didn't really know how to explain it well.

"So, you must really like her, huh?" Scarlett asked.

"Yeah. I think she's magic."

"You still believe in that stuff?"

I didn't believe in magic. But I couldn't think of another word to describe Mel.

"Besides, kid. If she likes you for who you are, then stay authentic while you still can," Scarlett advised as she pulled up to my place. "Get some food and come back later in the week."

"Thanks, Scarlett," I said as I got out of the car.

I knew Mel told me not to, but I couldn't help it. I was curious. I went into my bathroom and took off my clothes and stepped on the scale. Anxiety tightened my chest when I stepped on to see three blank zeros flashing on the screen before the numbers formed to 273.8. I sighed. I was disappointed. It didn't seem like enough.

I knew change didn't happen overnight, but I wanted to make traction already. I felt gross looking at myself in the mirror without any clothes, seeing my stomach pour over my waist and my fat chest that Lewis called "man boobs" one time. I was sick of it all. I felt so insecure and change needed to come sooner than later, so I went into my room and started doing leg lifts, planks, sit-ups, and everything I could to work up a sweat. As I got to around thirty sit-ups. My stomach didn't feel good at all — I was going to vomit. I rushed to the toilet and threw up everything. Well, technically only the protein bar. It hurt . . . a lot. I took deep breaths trying to calm myself down. I took a few moments to compose myself, then got off the floor and leaned against the sink to see my reflection in the mirror. I didn't look too great. My eyes were watery from throwing up, but I did see the scale past my reflection, so I turned around, took off my clothes again, and stepped on. I closed my eyes when I saw the three zeros flashing into something new — I thought about being skinny, being fit, being happy.

When I opened my eyes again, the scale said 272 pounds. It was lower, and at that moment, I was closer to being skinny than I was before. I needed to keep the momentum going. Food was difficult for me, I knew I would overeat, but I had to pace myself. I had to make a sacrifice. So, I started eating in the mornings and shortly before kick-boxing class. I did this for a few days. Everything felt a lot heavier, I was a lot more tired, but it worked.

Mel sat with me in the cafeteria the day Donny made his big return to school.

"Hey, hey," Donny said as he pulled up a chair. "Did you get a bit smaller?"

I blushed a bit. Maybe I did get smaller. I had lost around ten pounds.

"Yeah, he did!" Mel said.

"Who are you?" Donny asked, confused. He looked a bit taken aback by the fact that I was sitting with a girl.

"I'm Mel. Adrian's . . ." She wandered off in thought as she grinned at me. "I don't quite know what to call us yet."

I didn't know either. I did know she made me smile back, causing both of us to blush.

"I can take a hint." Donny laughed. "I never thought I'd be third-wheeling you, Adrian."

"Take a seat anyways. I've heard a bit about you," Mel said.

"Hopefully good?" Donny cocked an eyebrow.

"I heard about the time you peed yourself during a school camping trip in grade eight."

Donny's eyes widened.

"We're not supposed to talk about that." He looked at me seriously.

"I'm sorry." I burst out laughing. It was quite funny. Donny was my friend, but I couldn't help being amused. A few people looked over to see what was so funny. Everyone knew about the incident, but Donny wanted everyone to forget. He just sat there with a frown across his face.

"Did you tell Mel what your big pickup line was in grade eight, Adrian Carter?"

*Oh no.* I wasn't ready for that.

"Don't say anything," I said. "Seriously."

"It's too late, AC." He laughed. "Check this out, Mel. So in grade eight, Adrian had the biggest crush on this girl named Cassandra. He wrote her a love poem and everything."

"Oh. Sounds like things were getting pretty serious." Mel laughed and leaned her head forward.

"Oh yeah. They were." Donny gave me a grin. "Most of it was plagiarized lyrics from love songs, but this one line that he wrote all by himself stood out."

"Don't," I said sternly.

"Tell me!" Mel pleaded.

"He wrote: Adrian plus Cassandra, we can be an A.C. because it's about to get cool in here."

My face went straight down into the table while Mel was half laughing and half cringing at me. Donny completely lost himself in laughter. It was true. All of it. I'd rather not get into the details.

"Where's your lunch, anyways, dude?" Donny asked.

"Yeah, AC." Mel was still laughing. "Where is your lunch?"

"I forgot it," I said quietly.

"Dude, that's like two days in a row." Mel shook her head. "Want something of mine?" She took out her lunch bag.

"Nah, I'm okay. I'm not very hungry, anyways," I lied. I was very hungry. I wanted to eat everything in that lunch bag, but I couldn't allow myself to.

"Okay, Adrian. Lunch is almost over but text me if you're hungry?" She got up and kissed me on the cheek. "See you after school, AC," she whispered in my ear. I frowned.

"See you after school," I said with red cheeks.

As Mel walked away, Donny stared at me with wide eyes and a dropped jaw.

"Dudeeee," he said with a smile, "she's so beautiful."

"Yeah. She's pretty great. I met her a couple weeks back. Things just kind of clicked."

"Nice, dude. I'm happy for you. Kinda jealous. But more so happy."

The lunch bell rang which meant it was time for class. Donny and I went our separate ways.

That afternoon was kind of rough. I sat in Math class by the window with the sun shining right in my face — I could feel my empty stomach. I thought about Mel. I was going to work out with her after school . . . and hopefully make out with her and stuff. Kissing was kind of cool. I hadn't told Mel, but on the rooftop that night . . . that was my first kiss. Donny's first kiss was at thirteen and he would never shut up about it. He always made me feel like a late bloomer. Maybe I was, but I was slow and steady. I was on the path to feeling happy, and I wouldn't let anything stop me.

After school, I met Mel by the fountain outside the entrance of the school. Both her arms were crossed and she wore a grin.

"You really know how to keep a girl waiting."

"Sorry. I'm super tired," I explained.

"Too tired to work out?"

"Never," I replied.

"You hungry, dude?"

I *was* hungry. But I'd save that for later.

"No." I smiled. "I'm good."

"All right." Mel shrugged. "Let's go."

Mel and I went back to the park where we usually worked out. I was a bit slower than usual, and she noticed fairly quickly. "Hey, you seem out of it," she said as we stretched. "You don't seem very focused."

I wasn't. I kind of wanted this workout to be over with.

"I'm fine, just need to warm up a bit."

"All right." She took my word for what it was and we began.

She had me jogging, planking, and doing push-ups.

"C'mon!" she cheered during my push-ups. I was tired, but I kept trying to ignore it. My chest was on the grass, and as I forced myself up, I could feel her sit on my back, causing me to go right back down.

"Why did you do that?" I was irritated.

She laughed in my face and laid in the grass with me.

"Because you're adorable." She laughed again. Her laugh made the irritation fade away.

"You don't look like you're having a good time right now." Mel pointed out while lying in my arms.

I wasn't. This wasn't fun, but it was something I had to do. I was too tired to keep going, so I told her that I'd like to stop.

"We don't have to do this every day, you know. We're allowed to take a break every once in a while." She pinched a cheek. "Wanna go back to my place and cuddle?"

"Yeah, kinda." I couldn't hide my smile.

"Let's go." She pulled me up.

When we got to her place, I sat at the end of her bed. I wanted to fall back on the pillows and lose myself in my dreams and think of somewhere happy.

"Dude, are you sure you're okay?" she asked.

"I'm fine." I grinned at her.

"You should lie down. Let me spoon you for a while."

"Spoon me!?" I hopped up. "What is that!?" Okay, I freaked out a little bit. I had no idea what spooning was, and to me, it sounded a bit dirty and I wasn't into it.

"You don't know what spooning is?" Mel started laughing.

I didn't understand what was so funny. I mean, someone just said the phrase, "Let me spoon you," and it threw me a bit. I didn't know what "spooning" was. But I guessed I was going to find out.

"What is it?" I asked in a shy voice.

Mel laughed a bit harder. "Just answer this question for me. Are you a big spoon or a little spoon?"

I thought about that for a moment. I was new to this, and I didn't want to bite off more than I could chew, so I told Mel that I was a "little spoon."

"Then come here, little spoon." She wrapped her arms around me and laid back in the bed. My body followed. She turned me to face away from her and wrapped her arms around me while holding on tight.

"This is spooning," she whispered in my ear. "See? It's not all that bad."

It really wasn't. Her magic filled my chest again, and I felt at ease. She began whispering all kinds of things to me, all of it nice, all of it wonderful. She might have been a hard-ass, but she was showing me her soft side. She didn't show this side often, and when I got to see it, God, the only word I could think of was magic. Then she whispered to me, "Today, I wanted to tell your friend

Donny that you were my boyfriend."

My heart jumped five feet in the air. I never had anyone ask me to be their boyfriend before. I really dug the idea. I thought about it for a moment but not for too long. I told her, "I wanted to say that you were my girlfriend."

"Then what was stopping you?" she asked.

"I didn't want to go ahead without the okay from you."

Mel paused. I couldn't see her face, but I swore I could hear her smile.

"Look at you, being a gentleman."

"Will you be my girlfriend?" I asked.

"Yes, you fool." She squeezed me tightly. We cuddled for a long while, and she held on until I closed my eyes.

I woke up facing her. I could feel her breath tickling my face, and her body was against mine. Everything felt real. I kissed her forehead and she woke up. "Don't kiss my forehead, you creep."

"Sorry," I said. "I didn't mean to wake you."

"Don't kiss me while I'm sleeping, you creep."

She buried herself against me and held on. I held on for a while, too. She wrapped her legs around mine and said, "You're really awesome."

"I'm vaguely okay."

She pushed my head back and made a face. "Take a compliment, asshat."

My head was now facing my phone. I pressed the home button and the time said 8:53 p.m.

"Shit." I sat up. "I missed kickboxing."

"Oh no," Mel said while rubbing her eyes. "That's not that bad, though."

It was. I had to burn off calories and fat. I began freaking out because of it. I got out of her bed.

"Where are you going, dude?"

"Uhh . . . I have to head home," I lied. "It's getting kind of late."

"All right. Let me know when you get home, okay?"

"Okay." I smiled at her. She got up and gave me a really big hug before I left.

I didn't go home. I went for a jog. If I missed kickboxing, then I had to make up for it. I ran, and I ran, and I ran. I didn't want to tell Mel because I didn't want her to worry. She'd told me to take a break, but I couldn't. I jogged all the way to our school and all the way back to my house. It took me little over an hour. When I got home, my parents were already asleep. So I did what I had done the last few nights. I took off my clothes, stepped on the scale, and waited. The zeros flashed and I stared at them until I got a new number. 270.5 pounds. It was lower. That was all that mattered to me. I had so much worry that Mel would get bored of me if I stayed fat. I don't know why I was thinking about forever, but I knew I couldn't stay fat for much longer. Mel was beautiful, but I wasn't. What if she wanted a guy with six-pack abs, big arms, and who moved with confidence? That wasn't me. I was the complete 180 of that. I knew I had to change. I had to change even if I had to hide my methods. I looked over to the toilet and thoughts starting racing through my head.

*Do I really wanna be one those kids?*

*This isn't a boy thing.*

*This will help me make progress.*

I felt worried, overwhelmed, and trapped. I was trapped in my body and I knew I had to break free, so I lowered myself to the toilet. I would have been lying if I said that I'd never thought about it, but I think within the last few weeks I had been more desperate. I stuck two fingers in my mouth. It was graphic, painful, and afterward my throat really hurt. The small amount of food I ate that day was looking right up at me. I got up to look in the mirror and saw myself staring back with red eyes. It hurt. I stepped on the scale and tried again. The zeros flashed and changed to 270 pounds. It wasn't ideal, but it did what I wanted it to do. If it meant I would lose weight faster, then maybe that was the way to do it.

# CHAPTER 7
# 230 Pounds

I kept a routine. It wasn't a healthy one, but I didn't care. I ate once in the morning and once in the evening. Every night when I got home, I went to my bathroom and I purged. Some nights I would binge before purging. Afterward, my stomach and my throat would sting. I hated every second of it, but I kept cough drops close if the pain was ever too unbearable. Eventually, the days turned to weeks, the weeks turned to months, and over time the scale went from 270 to 265 to 261 to 240 to 235, and eventually, to 230. I had lost forty pounds. Mel didn't know what I did when she wasn't around, and I planned to keep it that way.

It was difficult. I wasn't getting any nutrition and it was affecting me — I always felt so tired and had no energy. I often lied and said I was tired because I hadn't been getting sleep. It did the trick, though. The numbers on the scale went down, and people complimented me often.

I didn't think I looked any different, if I was being honest. That was the strange thing about losing weight. Other people will notice before you do. I had been growing my hair, but it began thinning in some spots and I tried my best to hide that. People were more interested in my weight loss, though. I was so used to my body that subtle changes didn't really feel that different over time. One person who really noticed was Donny. When I saw him at school he was like, "Wow, man. You're going to be skinnier than me."

That had been after I decided to skip breakfast. I forced a smile but didn't really feel too great. Mel was in exam mode, so I was seeing her less at school, and she had to take a step back from our workout sessions. It was also starting to get a lot colder. Fall was an interesting time. It was daring to go jogging. The wind would leave us with a chill. I didn't want to slow down, but fighting nature is dangerous. Mel warned me about getting a chill and said if I got a cold, she wouldn't want to hang out with me until I got better. She couldn't afford to be sick during midterms.

As brave as she was, she always found it difficult to try to talk to her father about being in the elite class. She would play loud music, be unapologetic, and call out her dad's crap, but somewhere down that path, she was still afraid to tell her father that she didn't want to be in the elite class. We spoke about that a lot. She kept up her invisible walls; I told her it was okay to lower them every once in a while. But I didn't want to pressure her. I loved her, and I wanted to make sure that we did things at her pace.

"Did you tell Mel that you love her yet?" Donny asked

while keeping watch outside of the washroom after gym. I still didn't like locker rooms so he stood guard so that no one came in while I was exposed.

"No," I sighed.

"What's stopping you?" he asked.

*Fear.* I was new to all of this. I was new to love and feeling anything other than sorry for myself. I didn't want to ruin it.

"I'm not ready," I replied.

Donny let out a gross laugh.

"Ohhh. Look at little Adrian, too afraid to tell his girlfriend that he loves her."

"Shut up," I grumbled.

"Fine, whatever." He giggled.

I finished getting dressed and we left the gym. Donny seemed to be a bit jealous that I had a girlfriend while he didn't. Maybe it was a big brother thing, but it got pretty annoying. I was worried about Donny. Some of the folks in his music club would post on social media, "Not all men are trash! All girls are the same." I was worried that the behaviour of that crowd might rub off on him.

Mel told me one time, "Sure, not all men are trash. But a good amount of them are, and the ones who claim not be trash need to hold the ones who are accountable. Will you hold them accountable?"

I promised I would.

I learned a lot from Mel. I think the most important thing I learned from her was how to listen and not to speak to every issue that didn't directly affect me. I learned more that way. She really opened me up to new ideas that

I hadn't thought of before.

"Hey, back to Earth." Donny waved his hand in front of me. "You daydream a lot."

"I know." I shrugged.

"Hey, man, anyways I'm skipping the next class, need to finish the homework that's actually due in it. I'd ask if you want to come but I know you'd say no."

"You know me too well." I shrugged a second time.

"Ha, that's what growing up with you does to me. Text me later if you wanna chill during lunch."

"For sure," I said.

Donny left, and I made my way down the hall toward my locker. I could see students staring at me. Not in the "Oh my gosh, he's such a fat guy" kind of way, but in the "Wow. He lost a good amount of weight" kind of way.

I still felt insecure about my body. It didn't help that people stared. I made my way to my locker, but before I could even set eyes on it, I felt someone shove me.

"What's up, fatass?"

I knew who it was before I turned around and saw Lewis give me his signature stupid grin. He had been keeping his distance from me since the cafeteria incident. They even took him out of our gym class because they didn't want him or Donny around each other, and if Lewis was suspended once more, the school would have to expel him.

"Just because you're not as fat doesn't mean you're not a fatass," he snarled.

That didn't even make sense, but it still hurt. Even though I wasn't "as fat," I didn't like being called that.

I'd never understood why he took his anger out on me.

I wanted to punch him in the face, but I couldn't. I didn't know why, but I couldn't. I had been doing kickboxing for the last couple of months, but something about Lewis brought out enough fear and anxiety that it turned me into stone. I just stood there and took it.

"You might lose weight, but you'll probably gain it back anyways. You know you can't handle yourself around food. You're gross."

He began sticking fingers in my chest, pushing me back against the locker, making me scared.

"You're lucky you know Donny, otherwise I'd pound your face again. But right now, there's no one here to save you." He shoved me against the lockers as people in the hallway watched. "Big tough guy. Think because you're in karate or whatever, it means you can take me. I'd wreck you, kid," he threatened.

I finally found enough courage and tried to shove him back, but all he did was shove me harder into the lockers. It hurt. Learning to fight is one thing, but having the confidence to fight back is another. In that moment, I couldn't find the strength.

"Watch your back, fatty. Ever throw a sandwich at me again and I'll whack you," he warned as he walked away from me.

I kept my head down. I knew everyone in the hall was watching, but no one said a thing. That was the thing I hated about high school. We all went through the same shit, but no one wanted to help anyone else.

I skipped the rest of school and went home. I didn't care. I was so mad at Lewis — he showed everyone how weak and incompetent I was. I hated him, and I wished I had punched him square in his jaw. But I hadn't. What I did do was go into my kitchen, and start making a peanut butter sandwich. And no, I wasn't hungry. I ate two granola bars even though I was already full. I ate a bowl of cereal while my stomach was beginning to hurt. Food comforted me, but it wasn't what I needed. After I drank the milk from the bowl, I thought about Lewis, I thought about Mel, I thought about my body and how I was letting everyone down. I smashed the bowl on the floor and just screamed. It wasn't pretty.

I stormed upstairs and stepped on the scale. That morning I was at 229 pounds, but it read 233 pounds right then. I wanted to cry, but I held the tears back for a few more minutes. I dropped to the toilet seat and stuck my fingers in my mouth and forced all that food out. I could taste the dirty feeling in my mouth reminding me that I didn't want to be what I ate. My whole body ached after that, so I dragged myself to my room and laid in my bed. It was an off night for kickboxing, and I had nothing to do. I was still so mad at myself for not fighting back. I felt like a coward, and a lot of people saw it. I imagined if Mel saw it, she'd probably think I was a coward, too.

I laid down on my bed for a few hours feeling frozen until I heard my phone vibrate. I checked it, and it was from Mel.

**Mel:** Hey, I haven't heard from you all day. What's up, AC?

It always felt nice not having to be the one who texted first, every time I received one from her, I smiled.

I texted her back.

**Me:** Skipped school today. Super pissed off
**Mel:** What happened?

I didn't want her to know about Lewis, but I didn't think I could lie my way out of it. If she didn't hear it from me, I'm sure she would have heard it from somebody else.

**Me:** Lewis shoved me in a locker today and yelled at me. I'm pretty upset.

There was a long pause on her end, and it was pretty unsettling. Suddenly my phone started ringing. It was her. I picked up.

"Dude, are you okay?" she asked worriedly.

"Yeah," I told her. "No. Actually, no, I'm not. I hate him."

"I know, babe," she said softly. "It's okay to not be okay."

"I don't know what to do. I don't want to tell anyone. I don't want to look weak."

I didn't want to tell anyone about Lewis bullying me. I knew that if my parents found out, they would think I was weak, too.

"You're not weak, Adrian," Mel said, annoyed. "You're strong in different ways. You're motivated. That takes strength."

I knew she was trying to make me feel better, but it didn't help that I could see right through it. I knew no matter what she said, it wouldn't take away my anger. But I also knew that she was trying, so I gave in to it.

"I know. Thanks, Mel. I don't even want to go to school tomorrow."

"Then you don't have to," she told me. "But I'd be lonely if you didn't."

That got a grin from me, but it didn't quite erase my anger.

"There'll be other times to make up for it," I replied.

"There better be."

Mel might not have taken the anger away, but she knew how to get me out of the mindset that led me there. It would return, but right now I was away from it all.

"So . . ." I said.

"So . . . what?" she replied.

I wanted to tell Mel how much she meant to me that night, but I couldn't find the strength to open myself up like that. Sure, she knew about my insecurities and boundaries, but that didn't make it any easier. I was sure once those words were said, my heart would sink into my stomach. I thought if I said it, she'd at least say it back. But I wouldn't know if she meant it, and just that thought, wondering if she didn't feel as strongly toward me, made me close up.

"Anyways." She cut in. "I finished my third exam today. Last exam tomorrow."

"Nice. How did it go?"

"I think I did pretty well. It was Advanced English, so you know how it goes. How many quotes from dead white guys can I memorize? Turns out a lot."

I laughed out loud for the first time that day.

"That's the sound I love," she said.

She'd said love, and it made me feel good. Not enough to tell her that I loved her, but I kind of knew there was something there. In time, it would come out.

"But yeah," she continued. "Pretty sure my dad might surprise me with a car during Christmas. We can hit the road, go to the woods, and I can show you that lake sometime. I think that'd be pretty rad."

"It would be." I smiled at the thought.

"I'll keep you in the loop, babe. I have to go. But take the day off tomorrow if you need it. Just know I'll be around if you need to talk. I can make time for you, AC."

I cringed when she said that, and I could hear her laugh on the other end of the line.

"Got it, Mel," I sighed.

"Don't be so glum. Talk tomorrow."

She hung up and I laid back on my bed. Talking to Mel did make me feel better about the incident. There was someone out there who hated me, but there was also someone out there who loved me. I knew neither of us said it, but I could feel it. Maybe someday I'd find the strength to tell Melody that I was in love with her.

# CHAPTER 8
# Kickboxing Kids

I skipped school the next day. My parents had stopped knocking on my door to wake me up when I was fifteen. They said school was my decision. If I chose to go then I'd go. If not, then I wouldn't. Of course they gave me all the positive reasons as to why it was a good idea to go, but I needed a mental health day. I did plan on going to King's that night. Kicking and punching pads relieved a lot of stress, and I was getting really good at it.

Once I got there, I was already in full uniform because the locker room fear I had was universal. I walked up the steps toward the mat, and to my surprise, I saw Melody stretching her legs in a King's uniform. She didn't see me at first, but I looked around in a bit of disbelief and caught eyes with Scarlett.

"We got a new girl," Scarlett said excitedly. "We're in need of more women here."

Mel overheard that comment and looked up. She saw me standing next to Scarlett. "Hey, Adrian." Mel got up.

"Hey . . ." I waved to her.

I didn't know why she was there, and I didn't know if it was good or bad, but it was something that I couldn't quite translate for myself. It's weird when you live in two different worlds and then they suddenly collide. You don't necessarily think they need to be intertwined, but then it happens. I didn't know what to think of it.

"Hey. This was supposed to be a surprise for you. But I'm kind of not surprised you ruined it by being late," Mel said. "You didn't reply to my texts. Were you in bed all day?"

"Yeah. Pretty much. I was catching up on a lot of sleep."

"Get out of bed, lazybones." She winked at me.

"Are you that girl Adrian tells me about all the time?" Scarlett cut in.

Mel turned red and looked at me. "Yuck, probably. I'm Mel."

"Ahh, you are. This is exciting. I'm Scarlett."

They shook hands and made the crossover of my life official. As they began chatting, Ryan entered the gym and said out loud, "Everyone find a partner!"

I looked back and forth between Scarlett and Mel and felt really uncomfortable about it. Scarlett was always my partner for class, and I didn't want to let her down. She taught me a lot and I wanted to learn more. Mel was my girlfriend, and I felt like maybe I should be her default partner. But her showing up was really unexpected, and I didn't know what to do so I just kind of stared at both of them, until they made a decision themselves.

"Hey, wanna be my partner?" Scarlett asked Mel.

"I'm down," Mel replied.

My eyes widened in shock as they walked away from me. It kind of pissed me off.

I ended up finding a partner, at least. He was a new guy, a bit older than me. His name was Mitch. He had long, curly blonde hair. I'd only seen him here once or twice before, and he held up the pads very hesitantly. I was more focused on Mel and Scarlett, though. I listened in on their conversation.

"So, are you new to kickboxing?" Scarlett asked.

"To this form, yeah. I am a black belt in karate, though," Mel answered.

"That's exciting. You're gonna be fun to work with. Show me something fancy." Scarlett held out a pad.

"You got it." Mel stepped back, watched her distance, lifted her leg and brought it forcefully down. The impact could be heard all across the gym.

My jaw dropped. I never knew she could do anything like that.

"What an awesome axe kick." Scarlett was in awe.

"Hey, Adrian." I heard.

I turned back to face Mitch who was still holding out the pads.

"Show me a cool kick." He held out a pad. His hand was a bit shaky.

"All right," I said. I thought I should try to one-up Mel and look cool.

I stepped back, measured the distance like she did, and moved forward. I threw a kick but somewhere along the line Mitch flinched and moved backward, causing me to overextend myself and fall to the ground. Everyone saw. It was awful.

"You all right?" Scarlett walked over.

"I'm fine." I laid there for a moment. "Everything is wonderful."

Everything was not wonderful. I got back up, and Mitch managed to mutter, "Sorry," with his head down. I just shook my head at him.

At the end of class, I sat to the side of the gym filling my empty stomach with what was left in my water bottle. I had only eaten breakfast that day.

"Hey, superstar," Mel said as she approached me with Scarlett. They had a certain vibe to their walk like they'd known each other for years when they'd actually just met. It was like they were on the same wavelength. I wished it didn't annoy me, but for some reason it did.

"Mel did really great tonight." Scarlett put a hand on her shoulder. "She's stellar at kicking things."

"I try." Mel grinned. "Need help up?" Mel extended an open hand.

"I'm fine," I said, feeling a bit frustrated.

"All right then," Mel replied, looking confused.

I walked away and went straight to the washroom to avoid the locker room, then I realized I hadn't brought any clothes to change into, so I stayed in there and sat on the toilet. I was very annoyed that Mel was there and that she suddenly became the class badass while I knocked myself over. I could hear Mel and Scarlett talking outside the door.

"How long ago did you stop training in karate?" Scarlett asked.

"About two years ago. I've been training since I was a kid," Mel answered. "I always wanted to try to cross-train, but was recommended against it."

"Ahh, gotcha," Scarlett said. I walked out the door and butted into their conversation.

"You must be a bit rusty?" I interrupted

"Wait, you heard all of that?" Mel asked, a bit surprised. "And no. Everything felt super good tonight."

Okay, maybe that looked a bit weird on my end. Maybe you shouldn't eavesdrop on people and then intrude into the conversation.

"Anyways," Scarlett interrupted. "Would you like a drive home, Mel? I usually drive your boyfriend, but we can fit another person in there."

"Sure," Mel said. "Just let me grab my stuff."

As we walked outside, Scarlett and Mel were talking away about their different styles and training methods. As we got closer to the car, I called, "Shotgun!"

"Sorry, Adrian." Scarlett looked back at me. "The front is for my new homegirl," she said as she looked at Mel. Then the both of them broke out into laughter. I sighed and got into the back.

Scarlett decided to drop off Mel first because she lived closer to King's than I did. But during the whole car ride, it seemed to be a back and forth conversation between them about school. Mel told her about the elite class and how much she hated it. Scarlett was sympathetic and said, "I'm sorry, sis. Can I call you that? I feel like I'm a big sister already."

Jealousy filled me. Scarlett was supposed to be my big sister, not Mel's.

"Yes. I always wanted a big sister. I'm an only child." Mel's face lit up.

Once we made it to Mel's house, I got out of the back to get into the front seat. She surprised me with a kiss when she exited the car.

"I'll see you tomorrow, right?" she asked.

"Yeah. I'll be at school."

"You promise?"

"I promise."

"Good," she said and made her way inside.

"How romantic," Scarlett observed as I got into the front. She hit the gas and took me home. All she did was talk about Mel the entire drive. It was weird because I was the one who usually talked about Mel. I stayed silent and she eventually took notice.

"Why are you so quiet? You usually can't shut up after class."

"I'm just tired," I said hoping to derail the questions.

"Get some sleep, kid. That Mel girl is something special. Remember that."

I did. It still weirded me out how quickly those two bonded during a one-hour class. I tried not to pay it much mind, but I went to bed feeling a bit weird about it.

The next day at school, I was sitting on a bench outside with Donny during our lunch period, and I explained what had happened the night before.

"She's invading your space, bro," he told me as he took a chug of pop. "That's your space. Not hers. You need to have some personal time away from your girl, dude."

"I don't know, man. Maybe it's something I have to get used to," I said.

"No way." He burped. "You have to tell her to leave. It's not like you show up in her elite class sayin', 'What up bae. I'm here now too.'"

"I don't think that's the same thing." I shook my head.

"Close enough." He threw his pop can away. "Speak of the devil."

Mel waved to us as she made her way out of the entrance of the school.

"Play it cool. Remember to be straight up," he joked.

"Not the plan," I grunted.

"Hey, what's up, losers?" Mel said.

"Oh y'know. Just chillin'," I said.

Donny looked over and raised an eyebrow at me and started mouthing, "Say something."

I shook my head. Mel saw everything. "What are you two weirdos doing?" Mel asked.

"Just . . . I don't know. How are you?"

"Good. I have my last exam tomorrow. I'd invite you over tonight, otherwise," Mel told me.

"Ohhh," Donny squealed childishly.

"Can it, dummy." Mel gave him a stare, and Donny made a "zip it" sign across his mouth with his hand.

"Anyways, last night was fun. I wanted to surprise you with that because our workout routines are going to have to die down a bit with the weather getting colder."

It was true. I'd hate to have to wear a snowsuit while doing planks. Although it made sense, I wish she had given me some notice at the very least.

"I understand. You were awesome last night. I never would have thought of you throwing axe kicks and all that jazz."

"I told you I was a black belt in karate. I'm full of surprises." She shrugged. "Anyways, I only came down here to grab some food. I have to get back to studying. I'll text you later, hon." She waved and left.

"She called you 'hon'. Y'all are like a married couple already," Donny giggled.

"Stop."

"Okay, okay. I'm only playing."

I appreciated the support of Mel joining my class, but the reasoning didn't always get rid of jealousy. So it went without saying that something was still a bit off the next night when I saw Mel already at King's, stretching.

"That's your girl?" Mitch grinned at me. "She's super hot."

"Shut up," I said to him. I felt really light-headed and annoyed.

"Jeez, calm down, bro. I'm just saying —"

"Shut. Up." I stared at him.

"Sorry, bro. I didn't mean anything by it." Mitch backed away from me.

That was weird. I didn't know where the courage came from to tell Mitch to shut up. I was still pissed off at him for making me fall in front of the entire class. I wasn't going to let him objectify Mel.

"Seriously, Mitch. Do not talk about my girlfriend like that, or any woman in general," I said sternly.

I could see he was getting annoyed, so I stepped back

and let my own frustration out in a breath of air, and I told him to be better.

"Whatever," he replied, rolling his eyes.

I didn't want to be Mitch's partner after that, so I partnered up with Mel. Scarlett was asked to work with Mitch and help him practice some more basic moves. He wasn't doing too well in the class. Ryan wanted to start with no-contact sparring, so I stood across from Mel, whose hands were already wrapped. She asked, "Is this going to be awkward?"

"Probably," I replied. I thought that maybe last class she just looked badass on a fluke. There was no way she could consistently be that good after not training for years, even if she was a black belt in karate.

"Three. Two. One. Go!" Ryan called out. We began. I moved forward, fighting through the headache I'd had all day, and kept my hands up. Mel's hands were still lower than mine, but she came forward very fast. I threw a few punches close to her, but she dodged them swiftly and swung her hips into a kick, making her airborne. I moved back quicker than my feet would let me and fell back on my ass.

"Are you okay?" Mel asked, approaching me.

"I'm fine." I tried to stand up quickly so no one would see me, but as soon as I got to my feet, I felt really dizzy and had trouble keeping balance.

"I want to go sit down for a minute," I told her as I walked away from the mat. She was still that good, and my dizziness didn't help me either. I sat down and chugged some water, turned back around, and saw her waiting.

"Ready when you are," she said excitedly.

She seemed to really like class, a lot more than I did as of then. I hated how it made me jealous, but I tried to ignore it and walked back over.

"I'll go easy on you," she said.

We continued. I threw a kick, she moved her head back, and as I followed up and got closer, she threw a kick that landed right behind my knee. If she had used force, it would have taken me out and left me on the ground again. I readjusted myself and went for a lower leg kick, but she jumped right over it, and as I looked up she had her full leg coming down toward me. She threw another axe kick and I flinched, moving out of the way.

"We're only going easy, don't be so nervous," she said.

"Yeah, easy," I replied, knowing full well I was giving her all I had.

After class, Scarlett drove Mel and I home again. She dropped off Mel first and I got in the front after. Mel gave me a hug before leaving and Scarlett said, "Ewww. Keep it PG."

Of course she was joking, but Mel stuck her tongue out at Scarlett. "Stop being a prude!"

I smirked at that.

"See you tomorrow," Mel said as she walked to her door.

"Young love. I wish I had found someone in high school. All the guys I went to school with were dumb as a loaf of bread," Scarlett began saying as she drove off. "And, hey, dude, you found a really awesome partner."

"I mean, I guess."

"You guess?" Scarlett lifted an eyebrow. "What do you mean?"

"I mean, kickboxing was kind of my thing. Then Mel comes along and is suddenly the class badass," I told her.

"Men always want the spotlight," she scoffed.

"It's not that." I tried to defend myself. "I've been working at this for a few months. I'm supposed to be the one who is good. She took a break from martial arts for a few years, and suddenly —"

"Listen." Scarlett cut me off. "Jealousy is still jealousy no matter the explanation. You should be building up the woman you love. You should try to be better for her. Don't bring her down, dude. Like, how big is your ego? There's not many women at King's martial arts, haven't you noticed? Like, the place is called King's — it's clearly catered to men. Secondly, she is a damn black belt. I know you think you're being some badass because you've practised kickboxing for a few months, but she's been doing martial arts for half of her life. You need to respect that. If you don't, I'll eat you alive. Got it?"

"Got it," I replied instantly. I think it was at that moment I knew there was a lot of growing I had to do. Scarlett was right. I needed to inspire the woman I loved. We shouldn't take anything for granted.

I was silent most of the ride home and so was Scarlett. She drove up to the side of my house and reinforced her previous words. "Sure. What I said was harsh, Adrian. But you have to remember that you're not the victim here. Be good to Mel. Make her feel like she belongs. Because she does."

"She does matter," I said softly. "Thanks, Scarlett." I got out of the car and went straight inside.

When I got inside, I didn't weigh myself, I didn't take a

shower (which I probably should have), and instead I went straight to my room, turned off the lights, and reflected on what Scarlett had said to me. She was right. I loved Mel. I had to do better. I had to be better.

The next morning when I woke up it was 8:15 a.m. Class started at nine. I rushed. I couldn't find my water bottle, so I just ran for my bus because I couldn't be late for gym class with Donny first thing. I didn't even have time to weigh myself . . . or eat breakfast. I tried my hardest to make it on time but when I got off the bus it was already 9:12 a.m. So I ran into the school and straight to the gym. Donny was already there, leaning against one of the machines in the weight room as if he was too cool to be there.

"What's up, AC?" He smiled. "You look wiped."

"Yeah. I just ran here from the bus stop. I didn't want to be late."

"Well, you are. It's no biggie though. I guess I can't participate in gym today."

"Why not?" I asked.

"I'm wearing jeans." Donny pointed down. "I don't have the correct attire to use any of the equipment in here."

"Yeah. Like that wasn't intentional." I grinned. "What did Mr. Stephens have to say about that?"

"He just shook his head at me and walked away."

We both laughed. I could picture that scene in my mind, and I would have loved to see Mr. Stephens's stupid face while Donny gave him a smug look. I took a seat and we chatted for a bit.

"How's kung fu going?" he asked.

"You mean kickboxing? It's pretty great."

"That's not what you said a few days ago. Mel still going?"

"Yeah. She's doing pretty well, actually. Her karate experience really kicks in."

"Yeah, but is she still knocking your vibe? The other day you were saying how she made you jealous. Did you talk to her about it? Can she scrap, though?"

"Yeah, she kind of got the better of me last night. It was pretty embarrassing."

"I'm sure it was. She shouldn't be there," he said, before getting distracted by something in the corner of his eye.

I turned in the direction that had grabbed his attention and made eye contact with Mel. She was standing in the doorway holding the water bottle that I couldn't find earlier.

"Here's your water bottle, douchebag," she said in a low voice, dropping it on the floor. My heart fell and I didn't know what to do or say, but she was already gone.

"Well, that was awkward," Donny observed.

"Donny?"

"Yeah?"

"Shut the hell up." I grabbed the bottle and left.

I had to find Mel and tell her I didn't want her to leave King's, but I was afraid the damage was done. I knew she had a free period during my gym class, but I had no idea where she was. I checked her usual hangouts: underneath the stairs by the cafeteria — no luck; outside by the bleachers — also no luck. I sent her a text but I didn't hear back. I was starting to freak out. I felt like there was a ball pit inside of my chest and everything was being swooshed around.

The last place I checked was the library. I saw her back to one of the bookshelves. I could tell it was her because she was wearing her skeleton keytar button-up shirt. I walked up with a knot of worry inside of my heart and said, "Hey, Mel."

She turned around. She looked pissed when she saw me.

"Do you have something to say to me?" she asked angrily.

"Umm."

"If you're gonna say something, say it."

Wow. I was completely lost for words. We had never actually gotten into a fight before, so this was new territory for me.

"Yeah. Maybe. Can we go sit down somewhere?"

"Under the stairwell. Come on," she told me. I followed.

I tried to hold her hand but she swiped it away from me and said, "Not the time."

When we made it beneath the stairwell, she rounded on me. "Why didn't you just tell me? Why did I hear that you don't want me in your kickboxing class like that?"

"I do want you there," I said feeling tense. "When I said that to Donny, I was jealous."

"Jealous? Why?"

"Because you're really good."

"Oh, come on. You're upset because your girlfriend can do fancier kicks than you?"

"Fragile masculinity. I know," I sighed.

"That's one word for it, dude. I wanted to *help* you. We can't go jogging, we can't do stupid planks, and we can't do push-ups outside anymore. Winter is going to be here soon so it's too cold for that. I wanted to join the class and help motivate you. I also wanted to join because I miss it. My parents couldn't afford for me to continue karate after the divorce, so I was alone. I never really got over it. I always kinda feel alone, Adrian."

A wave of regret unfolded inside me. I wasn't fair to her. I didn't want to take that sense of community away from her. I knew she was lonely, and this could be good for her. She was right.

"I'm sorry, Mel. What I did was wrong and it was rude. Scarlett called me out on it and she was right. I told her how I felt the other night and she tore me apart."

"Yeah." Mel rolled her eyes. "I wish I could have seen it."

"Me, too. But, babe. I'm sorry. I don't want you to leave King's. You deserve to be there just as much as I do."

"You have to do more than say that. You have to take action."

"I will," I said. "Listen, I've learned a lot from you and Scarlett. And you're both teaching me things that I never would have thought about before. King's is a place that doesn't have many women. And we need to support the women in our lives. Mel, I appreciate you, and it wouldn't be fair for me to push you away. I have to handle my ego and get rid of my bad habits. But you're not one of them."

I could see her frustration beginning to fade. I continued.

"I need you close. You're not someone who I want to push away. I messed up. Full stop. You're someone who is helping make me physically smaller, but you're also making my heart bigger. This relationship has been good for me, and I hope it's been good for you, too."

"It has been good for me." She crossed her arms and sighed. "But you need to communicate with me, Adrian. I care about you, too. And if you still want me there, I'll stay. If you want me to leave, then I'll be a disappearing act. But you have to talk to me. Got it?"

"I got it, and I want you to stay."

"Okay," Mel said. "I'll stay."

"Thank you." I went up to her and gave her a hug. It took her a moment, but she hugged me back.

"I adore you, Mel. Thank you for everything."

"I'm thankful for you, too, even if you kind of suck sometimes," she said. "Thank you for being honest, but just talk to me next time. I know communication can be awkward, but I'm still your girlfriend. You're allowed to speak to me, even if it feels weird sometimes. Got it?"

"Got it," I said back.

"Good. I'll see you there tomorrow?"

"Yeah. I'll see you tomorrow." I smiled.

She shrugged back. Things weren't completely fixed, but it was a start. I clearly had more work to do.

But I did see her at the next class, and the one after that, and the one after that. Mel and Scarlett's bond strengthened over time. I was happy about that. At first, I wasn't, but things change. Maybe my many worlds coming together didn't make things more complicated. Instead, it made support so much easier, and the numbers on my scale kept going down through kickboxing . . . and other means. I still purged, and sometimes binged beforehand. It wasn't healthy. But it was my secret. I had to keep it close to the chest. Mel wouldn't be happy if she found out. But after every class, I would step on the scale and the numbers went down ever so slightly. It was still progress to me, and I knew someday I would be skinny.

# CHAPTER 9
# Cheat Day

"Wanna have a cheat day?" Mel asked when she woke up beside me. It was a late Saturday morning. She had stayed over after kickboxing the night before. We tried to do a sleepover once a weekend, either at her place or mine. That weekend it was my turn. My parents didn't mind her spending the night. My mom actually liked Mel a lot. She showed Mel all of my embarrassing baby photos and even gave her one. Baby photos made me cringe.

"Hey, I'm talking to you." Mel poked my forehead. "Wanna have a cheat day?"

"What's a cheat day?" I asked.

"It's when you take a day off from exercising and treat yourself with snacks and junk food. Honestly, I feel like pizza and chips, AC. Let's go to the grocery store. You've been doing so great. You deserve a treat."

It took me a moment to let that sink in. I didn't think I was a cheat day kind of guy; I barely ate enough as it was. Mel didn't know that though.

"Ahh, yeah, maybe. I just have to head to the bathroom first."

I got out of my bed, but she held on to my hand as I tried to walk away and said, "Let's spend the day together."

"Yeah. Let's spend the day together." I smiled at her.

I made it to the bathroom, I took off my t-shirt and shorts and jumped on the scale to watch the zeros flash in my face. I'd have a cheat day on one condition: If my weight was lower than usual, and it was. The scale said 226.5 pounds. That was a relief. I hadn't purged the night before because Mel was over, and I didn't want her to hear me. She couldn't find out about what I was doing.

I made my way back to my bedroom and laid down beside her.

"Let's have a cheat day." I smiled.

She smiled back, then stuck her tongue out at me. I stuck mine back out at her, then she flicked me, and I flicked her back, and then she found my weakness by tickling me. She started with my arms, and then ended at my stomach.

"Stop, stop." I pleaded playfully through the giggles, when really, my stomach felt sore when she tickled it.

"Fine." She smiled as she wrapped her arms around me.

We began playing with each other's hair, admiring our features, touching skin.

"We're both brown." She said. "But different kinds of brown."

She was darker than me. Deep down, I wished I were darker than I was. Being mixed was weird, for both of us. Mel and I related heavily because of that. I often times felt like I had to prove my blackness to feel comfortable in my identity. But I began to learn that there was no certain way to be a certain color, you just are who you are. The rest of the world didn't understand that though. I always found it weird that students at school thought I had to act a certain way to fit their expectation of being "really black."

Mel dealt with similar issues. Customers at the music shop she worked at would ask where she was from, even though her father had a Canadian flag incased behind the front counter. One customer even said, "Mixed people are so fascinating," when he found out that her father was white. It was weird. The world tried to fetishize and label people like us, they tried to keep us in boxes, but we were learning to break out.

"Remember that time we were on a date?" I asked.

"We've been on more than a few dates, Adrian," Mel replied.

"No, no. The one where we were sitting on the waterfront, and those bro-dudes came up to us." I sat up in bro-dude posture with my chest sticking out. "And that one dude was like, 'So like, my friends and I were like, wondering like, what are you guys?'"

"Yes! I shut him down real quick." Mel began to giggle while sitting up. "I told him 'Clearly not a fucking dragon, because I'd set you ablaze!'"

"His face was so red! And I was laughing so hard that I couldn't breathe!" I remembered.

We both broke into laughter. We were young, we were brown, and we weren't going to follow anyone's criteria. Loving Mel was an adventure that I never wanted to end. God, she was amazing.

She got out of bed and ate a bowl of cereal; I told her I wasn't hungry, but she stuffed about five granola bars into her coat pocket if I changed my mind on the way to the grocery store.

"We should get the bus," Mel suggested around noon. "It comes every half hour on the weekends, so we should probably be on our way."

"Sounds good to me."

We hustled to the bus. The grocery store that we were going to was called Cool Foods. It was about ten blocks away from my house, but the bus ride only took us five minutes. The C in the giant lit up sign hanging over the entrance needed some repairs since it read OOL FOODS. The store also didn't look super busy from the outside — only five cars in the parking lot and it was beginning to get cloudy. I could also see frosty air coming from my lips. It looked like winter was teasing us.

"Let's get inside, it's starting to get cold." Mel grabbed my hand and pulled me forward. When we got inside she grabbed a cart and said, "Wanna sit in? I'll push you around."

I laughed.

We skipped the fruit and veggie sections and went straight to the chips and chocolate.

"What do you want? All Dressed or Sour Cream and Onion?" Mel asked.

"You know I hate Sour Cream and Onion."

"How can you hate it? It's the best flavour. You're weird."

"No way. Sour Cream and Onion is very low in the hierarchy of chips. All Dressed is at the top, then it goes Dill Pickle, Ketchup, Barbeque, and then MAYBE Sour Cream and Onion."

"Dill Pickle? Gross, Adrian." Mel shook her head. "It goes Sour Cream and Onion, Ketchup, Barbecue, Salt and Vinegar."

"Salt and Vinegar!?" I gasped. "I don't even know you anymore."

As Mel and I argued over how the potato chip hierarchy should look, an older couple walked past us, staring. It took a few moments for us to realize, but once we did we both burst into laughter, causing them to scurry away.

We settled on ketchup. It was the most "equitable choice" Mel said, considering ketchup was close to the top for both of us. On the way out of the aisle, Mel grabbed a two litre bottle of Cola.

Next was the chocolate. Mel grabbed a bag of chocolate almonds, two giant milk chocolate bars, and a case of chocolate raisins.

"You're going all out." I examined our cart.

"Go big or go home, dude."

"We are going home." I laughed.

"Don't be a smart-ass."

I tried not to be. "Need anything else?"

"Chocolate ice cream."

We put it in the cart and went to the cash register to split the bill. It came to about twenty-four dollars, no biggie. We stuffed the food items in our backpacks but knew we had to get home fast before the jug of ice cream melted in mine.

"Wait, why is the ice cream in mine? It's gonna melt," I whined.

"Just deal with it," Mel replied.

We bussed back to my place and decided we would order pizza for later. Mel sat on my laptop looking through a menu.

"You into pineapple?" she asked.

"Not a chance."

"Seriously, babe? It's the best kind."

"No. Pineapple pizza is for people who don't flush the toilet after they use the bathroom."

"That's unfair. We always order what you want when we're at my place."

"I mean . . . You got to choose the ice cream. Maybe I can choose the pizza."

"Babe, we're getting pineapple on this pizza one way or another. We'll go half and half. What do you want on your half?"

I sighed. "Just pepperoni and salami."

"You're boring. But it's set in stone. We'll order it this evening. Let's just watch some movies for a bit," she said as she popped open a bag of chips and began munching away. I told her I'd save my appetite for later.

So we watched a horror film while waiting. They weren't as scary during the day. It was about teenagers who were supposed to be around our age, but they were being played by actors who were clearly in their thirties.

"Nobody at our school is that hot," Mel said as the main

character came on screen. He was a white guy with blonde hair and muscles. I was the polar opposite: black, chubby, and with curly hair.

"I mean . . . I'm kind of the opposite of that," I pointed out.

"You are," Mel confirmed.

I felt a bit self-conscious when she said that. But she continued by saying, "Though, those Eurocentric beauty standards aren't my desire if that's what you're getting at, babe. I'm attracted to you. The boy with the hair that refuses to fall flat, and with skin that is brown and beautiful, like mine."

She grabbed my arm and put it against hers to compare.

"Like I said earlier, we're both brown, but different kinds of brown. I find us to be illuminating."

I think that was the nicest thing anyone had ever said to me. I didn't even try to hide my smile. I gave in to her tug on my chin, and she kissed me. She kissed my face, and every time she did was a reminder of how awesome it was to be alive. It made me feel as if things were going to be okay.

After a horror movie and its sequel, it was six in the evening. Mel picked up my head from her lap and said, "Time for that pizza, babe."

She grabbed her phone and placed the order. As we waited, she opened another bag of chips and ate a handful.

That was it I guess. I was committing to a cheat day with Mel. I put a handful of chips in my mouth while feeling super guilty. It had been awhile since I ate any junk food, and the sweetness was stuck in my mouth.

"The pizza should be here in about twenty minutes," Mel said as she left my room to grab the cola.

The chips, chocolate, and cola that surrounded me made me feel nervous. To be honest, I didn't think I wanted to eat any of that food. Thinking about eating it scared me.

Mel came back in with the cola in one hand and the ice cream container and two spoons in the other.

"Let's get to business." She grinned.

I forced a smile. "Sure thing."

Mel opened up that ice cream container and went at it. It looked good, and I wanted to eat it. But habit kept me hesitant until she said, "Come on, man, don't make me be that person who's eating a jug of ice cream alone."

I managed a hesitant laugh and took a spoonful. The brown ice cream with chocolate chips poking out the top looked dreamy. I thought of it as a nightmare? I put it in my mouth and let it melt away. I took another spoonful, and another, and another.

Before I knew it, the doorbell rang. "Pizza's here!" Mel got up and ran for the door. "Don't worry, it's on me." She grabbed her wallet and went downstairs. I couldn't help myself. I kept eating spoonful after spoonful of ice cream. Mel opened the door with a pizza box in her hands and sat down on the bed beside me. She turned up the volume of my TV and began the third part of the horror movie. This time it was a whole new cast with not one, but two black characters this time.

Mel grabbed a slice of the pineapple pizza and put it close to my face. "See? It's not that bad."

"Get that abomination away from me." I swatted it away.

"Fine. Bask in ignorance, ignorant boy."

"Ignorant boy?" I laughed. "I like traditional pizza. Like pepperoni." I picked up a slice of my half and bit into it. It was warm, and I could feel the sauce and grease on my tongue. Wow. I missed pizza. It didn't take me long to eat a slice, then another slice, and another slice. Before I knew it, my half of the pizza was gone. So was Mel's. And we laid in my bed, bellies full. So she opened up the chocolate almonds, and we let ourselves feel fuller.

That morning, I hadn't expected Mel to spend the night again, but I just assumed she was going to. We were in my bed, and she was wrapped in my arms with sleepy eyes. It must have been the junk food.

I kissed her forehead, and I could see her crack a smile. "Adrian, it's okay to treat yourself once in a while. We can't always hold our urges in forever."

"You're right," I said.

She *was* right. But it didn't make me feel any better about it. Before long, the sun went down, and it didn't take long for her to fall asleep in my arms. Shortly after she did, I put her gently aside on the pillow and went into the bathroom. I stripped down to my boxers and stepped on the scale. I waited for the three zeros on the scale to change. I closed my eyes as usual, and when I opened them, my heart skipped a beat. Not in a good way — anger rushed through me. The scale read 231.9. I woke up that morning being 226. I had gained five pounds that day. I yelled at myself, but not loud enough to wake anyone up. I stomped my feet on the ground and kicked the scale to the side of the sink. I was so pissed off at myself. Why did I decide to eat that much? Why didn't I tell Mel I didn't want to do it? Why did Mel want to have a cheat day? Those thoughts were running through my head as I slumped on the ground. I didn't know what to do. I did the calculations, and even if I went to sleep with this much water weight, I'd probably wake up being at least 228 pounds. That was still a setback. I wasn't okay with that. I knew I had to do something drastic. I looked over at the toilet while I sat across from it. I ate a lot that day, and I knew it was going to hurt. A lot. I also knew that reaching my goal wouldn't be painless, so I had to. I got closer to the toilet and put my head over it. I put my index and middle finger in my mouth and reached as far back as I could until I felt a gag. My gag reflex was terrible, but I knew I had to fight through it and make it happen. I stuck my fingers deeper and deeper. I could feel the contents of my stomach rising up as I was gagging. It hurt, it hurt so badly. But I couldn't stop. I went deeper and deeper until it all came up into the toilet. I yelled after I did it. It wasn't as much vomit as I thought it would be. I knew I had a lot more food inside of me that I had to get out, so I dug deep again.

I did this until I threw up again, and then again. I hated every second of it, but I hated every second of looking at myself in the mirror, too. I hated every second of being made fun of at school. I hated every second of Lewis calling me a fatass. I hated every second of not being able to fit in the same-sized clothes as Donny wore. I remember when I was young, my mom had bought me all these back-to-school clothes. I was only about ten, but I tried them on, and none of them fit. I was too fat, and my mom hadn't gotten the receipts for the clothes to take them back, so she sat just there, crying. I could feel every tear coming out of her eyes. That was when I began hating myself. I was causing pain to other people. I hated myself to the point of not being able to stop eating. I would come home every day after school and binge eat everything in the kitchen because of others bullying me at school. It was an endless cycle, and food always won. I ate, and I ate, and I ate, and I couldn't stop. But right then, I vomited, and I vomited, and I vomited, and I couldn't stop. I couldn't stop until I heard the creaking of the bathroom door.

I'd forgotten to lock it, and that's when I saw her. Mel was looking at me while I had two fingers in my mouth. Her eyes were as wide as I had ever seen them. She had a look of shock as I stared up with vomit on my chin.

"Mel. Hi," I said, trying to stand up.

"Adrian, what the fuck."

"Mel, wait. I . . . my stomach."

"Why were your fingers in your mouth!?" she yelled. "Were you purging?"

"No. I wasn't," I lied.

"You were. You were!" She backed away.

"Okay," I said. I was caught red-handed, and if I lied again right then, it would be even worse. "Yeah. I was purging."

"Dude." Mel put her hands on her head. "That's so dangerous."

I stood up and grabbed a towel to wipe off my face. My

stomach hurt so bad. "I'm sorry. I freaked out after we ate all of that food."

"Adrian. Come back to bed. Right now, you need to lie down. We'll talk about this in the morning." I could see the tears forming in her eyes.

It was the first time I had seen Mel cry. Something hurt inside me when I saw it. The worst part was that I knew it was because of me. I'd let her down, and I could feel that weight rest itself on my shoulders.

I followed Mel back to the bed, and she slept on the side closest to the wall. I tried to put my arm around her, but she pushed it away. "No," she said, then turned her back to me. I think after a while she fell asleep. I turned my back to her, too, and I wanted to weep. But I didn't want her to hear me, so it took a lot to keep it bottled in. I was a mess, and it was beginning to show. After a while of fighting myself, my eyes shut for the night, and I went to sleep, too.

The next morning, I woke up and everything was a blur. I could see a sideways figure sitting on a chair beside my bed. I let my eyes adjust and saw Mel was sitting there, looking like she was ready to leave. She was staring at me.

"Adrian. What were you thinking last night?"

My memory came back in a flash. I remembered everything about the night before, Mel finding me on the bathroom floor, and I had no excuse.

"I'm sorry." I sat up feeling light-headed. "I ate all of that food and I went to the bathroom and I stood on the scale."

"You got on the scale? Dude. I told you not to do that. That number isn't accurate."

"I know," I said. "I can't help myself, though. I stepped

on the scale and saw that I was five pounds more than I was in the morning. I didn't want to do a cheat day."

"Then why didn't you just tell me?" She was furious. "Why didn't you talk to me? We spoke about this."

"I . . ." I didn't know what to say. "I don't know. I thought it'd make you happy if I did."

"Oh, shut up. That's bullshit. I found you last night with two fingers in your mouth, and you're saying that you're trying to make me happy? How long have you been doing this, Adrian?"

If communication was key, then I had to come clean.

"For a while."

"How long is a while?"

"Almost since we started dating."

I could hear Mel take a breath. She looked as shocked as if I'd hit her.

I continued. "Mel, I haven't been eating properly. At best, I have two meals a day and a lot of water in between. Most days I'm so tired and hungry that I feel like I want to pass out. I've been unhealthy about this whole weight loss journey. I haven't told you because I didn't want you to worry about me. I've been doing this because I'm tired of Lewis making fun of me, I'm tired of feeling insecure in my own body, and I'm doing this so you can have a boyfriend who looks good."

"I told you I didn't care what size you were." She stood up. "I don't care if you're bigger than most boys. That's not why I wanted to be with you."

She did say that in the beginning. She had said all of that.

"But I was wrong about you having an honest heart,"

she added. "You tell me that you've barely been eating food and then tell me not to worry? Adrian, the foundation of this entire relationship has been built on a lie. You can't excuse that. You lied to me, and you're hurting yourself. You are digging a grave, and you expect me to hold a shovel for you." Her anger turned into tears and I could see her starting to shake.

"I'm not going to watch you kill yourself to lose weight, you stupid boy."

Her tears began rolling down her cheeks.

"Mel." I got out of bed and reached out to her.

"Don't touch me." She swatted me away.

I stepped back and sat on the bed. "Adrian." She fought through the tears. "I can't do this."

Everything inside of me went sideways. It wasn't just anxiety that filled me now — it was fear. "What do you mean?" I started to get choked up. "What do you mean you can't do this?"

"I can't be with someone who is doing this to himself. I can't be with someone who is lying to me."

"I-I can change," I stammered. "I'll stop, I —"

"You've already broken my trust. This type of behaviour doesn't only impact you. For months, I've been trying to help you lose weight. I've given you advice on what foods to eat, I've been helping you exercise and get you healthy because I care about you. But this, this isn't healthy, Adrian. You are going to hurt yourself. You're going to do damage that you can't undo. Your body isn't going to adjust to losing weight like this." Mel stood up from the chair and grabbed her bag. "I'm sorry, Adrian. I know this is harsh. But I'm not going to be involved with this." She turned to the door.

"Mel." I stood up, too. "Mel, don't leave me. Mel, I need you!"

"What you need is to learn how to trust someone. What you need is to learn how to communicate with your partner. What you need is to not expect me to drag myself down into this hole with you. Adrian, I've lost enough people in my life. I'm not adding you to that list."

Mel left my room and stormed out of the front door. I followed.

"Mel, wait!" I pleaded. She stopped with her back facing me, but she turned her face back.

"If you're gonna say something, say it."

"I love you." I finally said it.

I was right, you know. My heart did sink into my stomach. I felt like I was left with radio silence. Her back was still facing me, but I could see her tense up. Her hand tightened into a fist. And she stood there for a few moments trying to fight back tears.

"Adrian, I . . . I loved you, too. But I can't continue to love someone who is lying to me, someone who is harming himself because they love me. I'm sorry."

Mel walked away and didn't look back. I stood there in a t-shirt and boxers, watching the girl I loved leave me. I felt empty, and not just because of the purging. Anxiety settled in my chest again — with reinforcements. It was all my fault. I had lied to her, and when you're not honest with someone, that hurts them. I couldn't hear her melody anymore. Her magic left my chest, and my heart was filled with what felt like stone. Later I learned it was depression. But in that moment, I felt lost in a sea of uncertainty. The light I followed no longer wanted to shine on me. I was left in the dark.

# CHAPTER 10
# New Body, Same Person

The purging didn't stop. It got more intense. When Mel left me, depression came knocking on my door, and it wouldn't leave. I quit going to King's. Scarlett would text my phone, asking me where I was but I never replied. I didn't even know if Mel kept going or not. I fell into a deep depression, and I felt like I was stuck in the gravitational pull of my bed. I barely ate and the purging had only gotten worse. Depression took away any motivation I had to exercise, and holding a spoon to my mouth felt like the heaviest burden I could carry. It was now March, and I wasn't a fan of the cold. Christmas had been hard. My entire family came over to our house, distant cousins, aunts, grandparents; we all fit in the clown car of my home. And every one of them commented on my appearance.

"Lookin' good, boy!" my Aunt Karen had said.

"Thanks," I'd replied. I wondered what she would have thought if she knew I had an eating disorder. My cousin Lance told me that I should "get into basketball," because I'm "lanky now." Sure, I was lanky, but I wondered what he would have thought if he knew how often I wanted to pass out from being tired.

The hardest part about Christmas was the food. My family went all out with turkey, ham, stuffing, buns, and everything else that you could imagine. I sat at the dinner table with a plate full of food and all I wanted to do was cry. I waited to purge until that night, when everyone was gone, and my parents were asleep. I was wearing an ugly Christmas sweater, not wanting anyone to see what was underneath.

I felt more fatigued as time went on. No food equalled no energy. I had an extra hard time paying attention in class because of that, even to the point where a teacher took me aside and asked if everything was okay. I told her that my imagination just got the better of me sometimes. It also led to dry skin, I used a lot more lotion than usual — I just told folks I was feeling ashy.

That March morning, I entered school and found it colder than usual. My hair was now a soft, curly afro, so it kept my head warm. But having less of a stomach made me chilly. I put my jacket in my locker and shut it. Underneath I wore a black long-sleeve sweater and blue jeans. I still didn't like showing skin. When I walked through the hallways, all eyes were still focused on me, but I kept my head down. I could hear whispers from students: "He got really skinny, really fast." Or, "I heard he got liposuction."

The liposuction rumour had been going around for some time, and it was bothering me. I didn't know why so many people cared that much to make stuff up. If I could afford liposuction, I would have done it. But even if I did, that wasn't anyone's business.

Later that day I walked down to the cafeteria and saw Donny sitting by himself. I pulled up and he said, "Wow, dude. Look at you dropping that weight. How much do you weigh now?"

"One hundred and eighty-five," I replied.

"Five pounds less than me. You could probably fit into this shirt off my back."

That was what I had wanted before this all began. But at that moment, I just wanted to go home and lie down. I was tired and hungry, but had a stomach ache.

"What did you bring for lunch?" Donny asked.

"I brought a peanut butter sandwich. I already ate it, though." I had no lunch.

"Those are always good," Donny said as he took a bite out of his burger. The smell filled my stomach and caused it to rumble. I sat there and watched him eat the entire thing. God, I wished I could have been that careless — eating a burger and not worrying about my weight afterward. Life wasn't fair, but we can't always change that.

"You've been really quiet lately, dude," Donny pointed out. "Not the normal, shy, quiet Adrian. You've been deadly quiet, like someone took something from you. Like you lost something. Maybe it's all that weight. You lost part of yourself." Donny chuckled at his joke.

I wished he wasn't right about that. I had lost a part of

myself. Something wasn't right beneath the sweater and the long sleeves that I wore. I covered up because I didn't want anyone to see what was beneath.

"You're allowed to say something, y'know?" Donny cut into my thoughts.

I forced a laugh to break the silence.

"Anyways, dude," he continued. "We should hang out soon. When you're not so busy with kickboxing."

Donny didn't know that I'd quit. He had no idea what I was doing to myself. I was afraid if he found out, he would leave me behind like Mel did. I missed her. I still saw her around school at times, but we passed each other like we were strangers. That was the hardest part. One second you love someone, then the next they're a disappearing act. Maybe that was what made love a magic trick. And I was feeling like the person who got sawed in half.

"I'm going to go upstairs and study for my math test," I told Donny. I honestly just wanted to get away from the smell of food. It filled my nostrils, making my stomach rumble.

"See you around, AC." Donny waved.

As I got up to leave, a guy stopped in front of me. I'd seen him around. He was in Mel's class. His name was Desmond. He stood in front of me, looked me up and down, and then just straight-up asked.

"Hey dude, is it true that you got liposuction?"

That question wasn't okay. No, I didn't get liposuction. I worked out for months with an amazing girl, fell off that wagon, and began purging/starving myself. But I couldn't say that. I was frozen. A girl who overheard the conversation looked over and asked, "Yeah. I heard you got liposuction, too. Can I see the scar?"

"I didn't get any surgery." I tried walking away. It seemed like every time someone asked a question, another person appeared, until I was surrounded. I was overwhelmed, and my heart began beating like a drum.

"Hey, come on, guys. Leave him alone." Donny stood up and tried to say something. His words got lost in the crowd.

"I NEED some weight-loss advice, Adrian. I've been trying to lose ten pounds since September," I heard.

"You're actually starting to look really cute," another said.

"What an inspiration you are. I mean, unless you got liposuction."

I hated it. My body wasn't a circus act. I was allowed to feel human. I didn't know what to say or how to reply. I wasn't used to any of it. I felt like my sudden wave of popularity was skin deep and the skin I was residing in at that moment didn't feel like home. I felt like I was standing in front of an audience, but didn't know my lines. I'd never liked attention, so it was weird. Most of the time when I got attention was when people were making fun of me, but this was different. People were treating me different ever since I lost the weight. It made my mind race and my stomach turn.

Nobody would back off, and I felt trapped. That was until I heard a loud whistle that grabbed everyone's attention. Everyone looked up, and there she was. Everyone's head turned to Melody.

"Listen," she said in a stern voice. "If he isn't respond-ing to any of you, leave him alone." Her words vibrated through the crowd.

"We're just giving him compliments, calm down," a guy said.

"Does he look like he's enjoying them?" Mel shot back. I was visibly shaking.

"Whatever," the guy replied. Shortly after the crowd died down.

Mel jumped off the table. She approached me, and I kept my head down. She looked at me like she didn't even know me anymore. When I did see her in the hall, her emotions seemed caught between anger and sadness. She was still angry with me for lying to her, but deep down I think she felt bad. I was still the same person. I just had a new body. Not everyone else knew that. Everyone else saw me as this inspirational superhero who defied all odds. In reality, I was ruining the only body I would ever have.

"You okay?" she asked.

"Fine," I said.

Mel let out a sigh and I stayed silent.

"Hey . . .uh," Donny said, "I'm going to leave before this gets awkward."

"Yeah. You do that, Donny," Mel replied.

Donny left, and there we stood.

I could feel Mel's eyes following up the sleeves of my arm.

"I only ever see you in sleeves now, you have excess skin, don't you?"

She could see right through me. She was right. I did have excess skin. I had a doctor's appointment the next morning about it. But nobody knew besides me. Not even my mom knew about it.

"Yeah. I have lots of it. I hate looking at myself."

"Are you still . . . ?"

"Yeah. A lot." I knew what she was going to ask.

"Listen, I was in a bad place that day. I was stressed with school, tests, and I . . ."

"I know," I said. "I should get going. See you around."

I looked up and caught eyes with her. She looked scared when she saw me. That was another emotion I had never seen from her before. We'd watched movies of people getting chased with axes, jump scares on the Internet, and she reacted with laughter. But if seeing me in this state was the only thing that ignited fear in her, then maybe I was a monster.

"Bye, Adrian," she said softly as I turned and walked away. The school bell rang and I got lost somewhere in the noise.

\*\*\*

That night I didn't purge. I went to the bathroom and looked at myself in the mirror. I took off my shirt, and I could see my skin fold and drip over my waist like it was clay. I wanted to be beautiful. But that wasn't beautiful. That was what monsters looked like. My skin was so stretched out across my stomach, chest, and both my arms. It was like I had wings, but I didn't feel like a superhero. A few months ago, I wanted to be able to take my shirt off at the beach, but right then I was afraid to wear anything besides layers and long sleeves. It was like my old body was a ghost that was haunting me. I didn't know how to fix it. I was broken, and I felt trapped. I just wanted to look beautiful.

# CHAPTER 11

# Excess

The next morning, I sat in the waiting room of a hospital with a ticket that read forty-seven on it. Out of all the people in that waiting room, I was number forty-seven. I was supposed to be in school, but I took the day off without telling my mom. She wouldn't find out. She was on vacation with my dad in Yarmouth. If the school called, I would delete the message they left on the answering machine. I sat there worrying about everything. I was also tired and couldn't focus on anything. My stomach was on empty and I was exhausted. I had to lean against the rail as I walked to the waiting room earlier. Folks walking by must have thought I was sick. A nurse walking by asked if I needed help, I waved him off. I didn't enjoy the attention it brought.

I was worried that I would need surgery, I was also

worried about whether the surgery for my excess skin was covered under my parents' health insurance. I had done some research about it and found out that unless my excess skin was causing me other illnesses, then it wouldn't be covered. It was. It was causing me to feel depressed, it was making me feel gross in most of my clothes, and it hung from my stomach, chest, and arms. I thought there would be a chance I'd hear good news, so I kept my fingers crossed.

As I waited, I could smell the freshly mopped floors. It was pretty early, around eight-fifteen in the morning. I could also hear a lady across from me humming in a soft voice. It made me feel at ease. Outside the waiting room, a man who looked three times my age barged in and began causing a ruckus about a vending machine not working.

"I put four toonies inside that thing, and not one cookie came out."

*Well, maybe he should have known it was broken after putting in the first toonie*, I thought. There was also an elderly woman with her walker, wandering around the waiting room asking where her mother was. It hurt to see. I didn't need a university degree to know what was going on right in front of me. Waiting rooms were rough.

I thought the weird part about being there was that I was alone. I was too embarrassed to tell my mom about it. I would never mention anything to my dad, either. I had to make the appointment myself from my family doctor. I needed his approval before I could see a surgeon. I got it. My family doctor had told me that I had lost all that weight too fast and that I was unhealthy. He told me that

I lost weight quicker than my body could keep up with or adjust to. That was why I had so much excess skin.

I eventually got called into the surgeon's office. It was well past eleven before I heard the secretary at the desk yell, "Forty-seven!"

I stood up and waved to her.

"Right this way." She got up and walked me to the surgeon's office. Once we got there, she passed me a nightgown and told me to put it on.

Hospital nightgowns are awkward. They have nothing covering you from behind, so I kept my boxers on and took off my shirt and pants. I sat there and waited, feeling very vulnerable. It wasn't long until the doctor walked in. He was a young man who looked like he should have been an actor in a soap opera. He was tall, with jet-black hair that looked like it waved in the wind. His dimples were very visible on his face. He must have been straight out of med school.

"You must be Adrian Carter," he said while looking at his clipboard.

"Yep. That's me," I replied.

"Hi there. I'm Dr. Johnson." He extended a hand. We shook. "So, your family doctor, Dr. Paul, says you have excess skin?"

"Yeah. I have a lot of it."

"Can I see?" he asked, writing on his clipboard.

I felt really uneasy about it, but I opened up my robe. It was the first time I'd shown anyone what I looked like underneath my clothes. I felt exposed, but the doctor didn't seem to judge. He just examined me like I was a puzzle for him to solve. He grabbed hold of my stretchy skin, and it sent a sudden shock up my body. His hands were so cold. *Why are doctor's hands always so cold?* He let go and asked, "Has this skin been giving you infections?"

"Infections? No," I replied.

"Hmm . . . Does it cause any discomfort? Do you get any weird itches or anything?"

"Itches? Not so much. But it does cause discomfort. It impacts the clothes I wear, and it's not good for my mental health," I explained.

"Mental health? What do you mean?" he asked.

"I've been really depressed because of it, and this skin isn't helping my confidence whatsoever."

"I see," the doctor said. "Hmm."

He grabbed my skin for another moment, looked me up and down, then finally let go.

"If you want to get rid of this excess skin, you're going to need surgery. We're going to have to cut from here, to here," he explained as he pointed from under my nipples to just below my belly button in a square formation.

"After that, we are going to have to pull your skin down and stretch it."

"What about my belly button?" I asked.

"We'll have to make you a new one. This one would just be medical waste."

That sent a shiver down my spine. I had that belly button my entire life, and, apparently, it would be considered "medical waste."

"Do these types of surgeries get covered by health care plans?" I asked.

That was the question I'd wanted to ask the entire time. I knew I wouldn't be able to pay for surgery because it could cost thousands of dollars, so I put my heart on the line.

"Unfortunately, no," the doctor replied while writing some more in his notebook.

No? How could he say that without any sympathy? He was still writing in his notebook and didn't even look me in the eye. It was my body we were talking about, and he didn't seem to care.

"How much would it cost?" I asked. I could feel my throat beginning to clog up. *I'm not going to cry*, I thought.

"Hmm . . ." He paused to think. "It depends. But just to ballpark here, I would say at least eleven grand."

Eleven grand to get rid of my excess skin. When I heard that, everything just kind of stopped. It made me think back to all the hard work I put in at King's, all of the nights Mel and I had gone jogging, all of those times I purged. All of my dreams of being shirtless at a beach, or being able to wear a t-shirt, just a plain t-shirt with no layers or sweaters. All of those memories and dreams got washed away in a hurricane. I'd said no crying, but I couldn't fight it.

"Yes." Dr. Johnson watched me cry. "These surgeries can be very expensive. But that doesn't mean you should give up. I read your file. You lost a lot of weight, and you did it for good reason. I don't see enough young men like you. I see young men who don't make the change, and those young men often don't make it past the age of forty-five. Don't let this obstacle stop you."

"How can I not let this be an obstacle for me!?" I sobbed,

wiping furiously at my tears. "I worked my ass off just to feel normal, and now I look like this! Most of my body seems to be medical waste. And this is what this whole mess has felt like, a big waste of time." I couldn't stop crying. I felt beaten and broken. I felt like I wasn't good enough.

I put on my clothes. Dr. Perfect Asshole didn't say anything and just watched me leave. I walked into the hallway, and tried to hide my tears, but it didn't matter. My emotions got the better of me, and I could see nurses and patients staring at me. They stared at me exactly how everyone at school stared at me. It felt no different. I ran into a washroom and all the eyes staring at me followed. As I ran, I felt something fall out of my pocket, but I didn't care. I slammed the door, locked it, and screamed. I screamed so loud that nobody could call me the quiet kid anymore. I was tired of being quiet, I was tired of hiding my pain, and I had to let it out.

I heard a knock on the door. "Sir. Sir, are you okay? You can't scream like that in there."

I didn't answer. I just slumped against the locked door and put my head in my lap. I sat there and cried.

It made me think back to a time with Mel. *You're allowed to cry y'know?* she told me that day in the park after those guys made fun of me. I'd been so embarrassed. *It's okay to cry, y'know. I know you boys don't like doing that much, but you don't have to hide your feelings here.* I could hear her voice.

The thing I loved about Melody was that every time I cried, she didn't push me away or tell me to stop. She held on tight. So, I cried there in the bathroom. I cried for all the times I hadn't allowed myself to.

I was in that bathroom for about forty minutes. Every now and then I could hear someone knock on the door, telling me to come out, or hear the doorknob twist and turn. But I just sat there, and soon enough all the knocking and the twisting stopped. At that point I didn't know how long I had been in there anymore. I didn't want to ever leave. Suddenly, I heard a noise that sounded like paper ripping followed by scribbling. Then a white piece of paper made its way beneath the door. I grabbed it, and it read: *Are you okay, AC?*

Then a pen rolled under the doorway, too. Only two people called me AC. That was Donny and Mel, and this didn't seem like an approach Donny would take.

I grabbed the pen and wrote back.

*No. No, I'm not okay.* And slid it back under the door with the pen.

What was Mel doing there? Why did she care? She had already left me when I was beginning to fall apart.

*I need you to come out,* the paper read as it came back to me.

*I don't want to,* I wrote back.

*I know. But we're all scared, and we all care about you.*

*Then why did you leave?* I wrote back. There was a long pause. I could feel pressure hit my side of the door. I could only assume that she sat against the door, too.

*It's complicated,* The note came back.

*I got time,* I wrote back.

*This isn't why I'm here.*

Before I could write anything, I realized that she didn't send the pen back. But I heard another page rip followed by more scribbling. It took a few minutes before she sent it. I picked it up and read it.

*Adrian, I'm sorry I hurt you. I really, really am. But I still care about you. I still want you in my life. I want you to be close. I know what happened. I know that you purge. I know that you feel awful that you have so much excess skin. But you have to know that you're still you. You're not everything on the surface. You're what's on the inside. I know, the inside is filled with pain, filled with so much sorrow, but you can rise above it. I believe in you. Donny believes in you. Scarlett believes in you. Ryan does, too. Sometimes you need to hit a low before you can aim high, and Adrian, I got you. We all have our faults, but that doesn't mean you're hopeless, it means you're human.*

*I'm human.* When I read that, my heartbeat brought me back to reality. She was right. I was allowed to love myself through the faults. It was something to work on. I got to my feet and looked at myself in the mirror. All I could see was skin, but beneath that skin was so much more. It's not easy to find confidence — sometimes it's something you need to build. As much as it took me to change myself on the outside, I knew in that moment I would have to use that same amount of energy to help fix what was on the inside. I grabbed the door handle and twisted it slowly. There she was. Mel stood in front of me. I still had tears rolling down my cheeks, and we stared at each other for a moment, then like a sudden rush, we embraced each other with open arms. I held on to her, and she held right back.

I lacked so much energy that she was almost holding me upright.

"I'm so sorry," I cried.

Behind her I could see three nurses all standing around the corner.

"He's finally out," one of them said, followed by a sigh of relief from all of them.

"You really know how to make a scene," Mel told me as she let go and helped me gain my balance. She looked really concerned. "Dude, you can barely stand —"

"How did you end up here?" I cut her off.

"Your wallet fell out of your pocket when you ran to the washroom. You still had that piece of paper I wrote my cell number on when we first met. One of the nurses called me instead of calling security."

Wow. I had totally forgotten that her number was still in my wallet. It was stuffed beneath my bus pass.

"Come on." She grabbed my hand and we left the hospital.

# CHAPTER 12

# Mosh Pits and Fragile Men

Mel bussed with me to make sure that I got home all right. On the ride home, I could barely sit up straight. I was so tired and tried my hardest to stay awake. I felt Mel put a hand on my shoulder. It was so gentle, but real heavy at the same time. She tried to force a smile, but she could see right through me. She knew I hadn't slowed down with the purging.

Once we got to our stop, she linked my arm with hers and walked me back to my house. She didn't say anything; I knew she wanted to. When we got to my door, she let go as I balanced myself. I was ashamed to look at her, but when I did, she had an extended fist toward me.

"Friends?"

I knew I would find it hard to stay only friends, but Mel was someone I cared about deeply. So I extended my fist and bumped it against hers.

"Please eat something, Adrian," she said.

"I will," I lied.

"All right." She made her way back to the bus stop, and I headed inside.

I settled myself in my bed and thought about what Mel said to me about "being more than the surface." I knew that there was still so much work to do. I fell flat on my back, feeling stuck in the gravitational pull of my bed again. I laid there all day, just thinking about what had happened at the hospital and all the extra folds of skin that I was left with. It was strange, I felt uncomfortable in normal day-to-day life while being massively overweight, and now, when I was skinny I still felt uneasy.

I laid in bed until I could see the moon switch shifts with the sun and soft light splashed through my window. There weren't many stars out that night, but I saw my phone light up with a text.

**Mel:** Dude. I know you've been in bed all day.

**Me:** How did you know?

**Mel:** Because I know you. And you just admitted it.

**Me:** . . .

**Mel:** You need to get out of the house. Wanna go to a show with me tonight? There's probably going to be a mosh pit!

**Me:** That sounds . . . great.

She had told me about mosh pits once, how everyone was crammed together, sweaty, dancing, yelling . . . it was the stuff of my nightmares.

Mel didn't text back. I just assumed she forgot about it. That was until I heard a car horn honking outside. I jumped out of my bed, startled. I ran downstairs and saw high-beam lights flashing through my living-room windows. Was someone honking their horn at my house thinking it would move out of the way? I didn't understand until I opened the front door. The light was so bright that I couldn't even see the car. Eventually, the light died down, and I saw a beat up, old school, faded purple Camaro. The front door opened, and Mel got out to lean against it while pulling her hairband off to reveal her new look. Her hair was long, natural and unapologetically wavy. She had on her black leather jacket and blew a ball of bubble gum from her mouth, followed by a pop.

"Your hair looks awesome!" I said.

"I know. You coming to this punk show or what?" she asked.

"A punk show?" I said, confused. "I'm not even dressed."

"You got five minutes." Mel reached into the car and honked the horn. "You don't want me to wake your parents, do you?" She honked again.

"They're on vacation."

"Neighbours then?" She honked louder.

"Fine! Hold on."

I rushed inside. My aesthetic didn't exactly scream punk rock, and I felt pretty insecure when I wasn't wearing anything dark. So I put on a pair of dark blue jeans and a baggy black hoodie.

"Where'd you get this car?" I asked, amazed.

"It was my Christmas gift. I told you I had a feeling my dad was getting me a car," she said as she got in.

"Your outfit isn't really screaming 'punk rock,' Adrian," she pointed out when I got in the passenger side.

"I know. It's all I got." I shrugged.

"It'll do. Let's go."

Mel put the car in reverse, and then we were gone.

Her car was a little messy on the inside. Schoolwork flooded the backseat, and there was a gym bag under my feet. Mel's phone was connected to an AUX cord, playing heavy metal. I wasn't a fan, so I spoke over the music.

"So where are we going?" I asked.

"There's a punk show in Dreamer's Corner. That's in the basement of Redemption House."

"Isn't Dreamer's Corner a bar? We're sixteen, we can't get in."

"I know a guy."

Mel turned into the parking lot. A group of bearded guys wearing either jean jackets or vests started cheering when they saw the car.

"What a beauty that thing is!" I heard one of them say.

"Let's go." Mel got out. She ignored the guys' questions about the car and walked right up to the stairwell that led under Redemption House. There was a giant of a man standing in front of the entrance. He had a big beard, bald head, and little patience.

"I'm gonna be straight up. I can't let you two in," he told us.

"I know the band playing tonight," Mel replied.

"Yeah, so? They don't get to let minors in a bar. Beat it," he sassed us.

"But —" Mel tried. She couldn't think of anything. So we were stuck.

Luckily, for us anyway, there was a loud smash from up the steps, and someone yelled, "Arg! He just bottled me! Get him!" Followed by scuffling and lots of cursing.

"Oh, dammit!" the security guard said as he rushed past us up the steps.

"Adrian, get inside!" Mel grabbed my hand and pulled me into the bar.

Red lights filled the atmosphere, and loud music went straight into our ears. I could already feel a headache starting.

"Hey! There's Desmond singing!" Mel pointed excitedly.

I could see Desmond on a stage at the opposite end of the room. It was the guy who asked if I had gotten liposuction. He was with an entire band of people who looked much older than him. I couldn't hear a word he was singing. It just sounded like screaming. I followed Mel into the crowd but got lost. Suddenly everyone started shoving each other. I felt someone bump into me, and I got slammed on my right side. I hit the floor. I was very confused, but before I could register what happened I heard people saying, "Help him up!" And two people pulled me to my feet then shoved me back into the action.

"MOSH PIT!" I heard one of them scream.

So this was a mosh pit. It was exactly as appealing as I thought it would be. I tried to make my way out of the crowd and get to the side, but people were falling over, being pulled back up to their feet, and I was running out of places to step. I kept my head down and basically crawled to one end of the room.

When I made it to the wall, there was a man who looked a bit dazed. He looked me up and down for a few moments and asked, "Are you the guy?"

"Am I the guy?" I replied.

"Yeah, are you the guy?"

"I don't know. Why would I be the guy?"

"Well, you look like the type of guy who is selling weed."

*Classy.* "Not every black person sells dope," I snapped as I walked away.

He became super defensive about it. "Oh, shit, that's not what I meant! I meant it because you wore a hoodie! I swear!"

I walked closer to the stage from the sidelines, and I could see Mel dancing to the music. She looked so free and like she was in her element. Seeing her dance like that made me crack a smile. As I tried to walk closer to her, a random lady came up to me. "Oh my gosh, can I touch your hair!?" she asked. She was already reaching for it.

"No," I said, blocking her hands.

"Oh, come on. Please? You're so handsome, I just want to touch." She kept reaching while I kept holding her hands back. It was an awkward struggle, and she wasn't taking no for answer. Suddenly she was shoved away by Mel.

"He's not a petting zoo, lady."

The lady's face went from being pale to bright red, and she hurried away.

"Are you okay?" Mel asked. "I looked over and saw that lady trying to grab your hair."

"Oh, yeah, the night's been fun. Got shoved to the floor, some dude thought I was a dope dealer, random lady tried to grab my hair. Mosh pits are awesome."

"Stick with me then. I'll punch anyone in the face who tries to annoy you." She grabbed my hand and pulled me through the crowd. We made it right in front of the stage and I could see Desmond's sweat falling from his face.

"Dance!" Mel yelled as she started moving her body with the music. I was too awkward for dance floors. Even at school dances, I stood against the wall most of the time. I still found dancing weird. Even being smaller, I still didn't feel confident enough in my own body to move with a beat. Mel grabbed my hands and started moving my arms up and down just like in her bedroom so long ago.

"Like this! Don't overthink it. Move your hips a little bit. There, you got it. Keep doing that. Be fluid. Fall back into the music. It'll catch you."

I trusted the music. It was pretty punk, but I was beginning to dig it. I had never danced in public before, so this was new, and a bit exciting. Mel cracked a smile at me, and I showed one back. We got lost in the music for a little while.

Things eventually died down, and people began to leave. Mel and I slowed, and I began to catch my breath. Desmond jumped from the stage and greeted us.

"Hey, Mel." He smiled. "Adrian." He nodded.

I nodded back. Ever since the liposuction comment, I got weird vibes from Desmond.

"Desmond!" Mel gave him a hug. "You were great tonight. Seriously."

"Thank you. I'm glad that you were here. The staff wants to clean up, so we have to leave. But I'm having a small get-together at my place. You two wanna join?"

"Heck yeah, we do," Mel said.

"Awesome. These are my bandmates by the way, Steph and Derrick."

Steph had purple streaks in her pitch-black hair and a jean jacket full of patches that said everything from, "save the environment" to "punch racists."

"Hello, younglings," was how she introduced herself.

Derrick had a green Mohawk and wore a denim vest. He was tall and super lean. He seemed like the tough, quiet type. They both looked at least five years older than Desmond.

"Wait, you're only sixteen. How did you get to perform here?" I asked.

Desmond smirked, reached into his pocket, and flashed me a card. "Fake ID. Hard to come by, easy to fool venues with."

I disliked how smug Desmond was. But there was no way I was going to let Mel go to his place without me.

Once we got outside, Mel made headed toward her car, but Desmond insisted that he only lived a few blocks away, and that it was better to keep her car there.

"You don't think it'll get broken into, do you?" Mel asked worriedly.

"What are they going to steal? The Iron Beard records in your backseat?" Desmond laughed.

I frowned. Mel glanced at me and laughed awkwardly.

"Let's just walk, okay?" she said.

I shrugged.

We made our way to Desmond's place. It felt really weird. I was walking behind Mel and Desmond while they took up all the space on the sidewalk. I didn't like Desmond, and I didn't like how he was walking with Mel, and I didn't like how I was only an afterthought. We walked for about fifteen minutes until we made it to some big white house, which was pretty close to the South End.

"Here it is!" Desmond said proudly. His place was huge. It had giant bushes that engulfed the gates, and a path that led to the front door of his three-storey home.

"My parents are asleep, but the walls are thick. We can all chill in my basement. Right this way." Desmond opened the gate to the pathway, and we followed.

Desmond's house was even more massive inside. He had mentioned that his dad was a banker and his mom invested in stocks and created apps.

"All right everyone, shut your trap until we get to the basement," Desmond whispered. "And yes, Derrick. You can smoke in the basement."

Derrick grunted. Desmond seemed like a real estate agent as he showed us his marble floors, flat-screen TV in the living room, and a china cabinet in the kitchen. This guy had it all. I felt overwhelmed with jealousy because I never had anything like this, but there I was just viewing it all like a tourist.

"Down this way." Desmond opened a door to a set of stairs and we all followed him down.

His basement had hardwood floors, a pool table in the middle, and leather La-Z-Boy chairs for all of us to sit on. As we got situated, he opened up a mini fridge and offered all of us beer. Mel and I both declined. For me, it was because underage drinking PSAs were burned into my brain. For her, it was because she had to drive home later. Desmond shrugged, popped open a bottle, and started drinking away. His of-age friends accepted a couple of drinks and sat back.

"Why don't you ever bring more of your friends from the bar over?" Mel asked.

"Ha, because most of them are in their thirties."

"Derrick is twenty-seven," Steph pointed out.

"He's got three more years until his midlife crisis. Until then, he's good."

"Ageist asshole," Steph growled then drank.

Derrick grunted as he lit a cigarette.

"Tell me about you, Adrian." Desmond switched gears. "Did you get liposuction or something? This kid lost like half his body weight."

"That's impressive," Steph said. "You don't talk much, do you?"

I looked over to Mel, and she gave me a nod. "I don't think he wants to talk about that," she said.

"Oh, come on. I invite this kid into my home — he at least owes me an explanation. What was it? If it wasn't liposuction, did you jam those fingers of yours in your mouth?"

"That's enough," Mel snapped. "Leave him alone."

"Yeah, don't be such an ass, Desmond," Steph added.

"I'm just saying what I heard from Lewis." Desmond shrugged.

"Lewis is an idiot," Mel huffed.

"You're right. But still . . ."

"But nothing," I finally said. "I lost weight from kick-boxing. That's it."

Lying was the only sensible way out of this conversation, but it only opened up more awkward subjects.

"So, you must be able to throw down, right?" Desmond asked. "You seem super timid, a bit fragile."

*Wanna see how fragile I can be?* Of course, I didn't say that out loud. I kept quiet because I knew better. Desmond sat back in his chair and continued to drink. I didn't understand why Mel was friends with this dude. He just seemed like the kind of pretentious person that Mel tried to avoid. He was rude to his friends, but they seemed to put up with him because of his fancy house. The dynamic of their friendship was very strange.

Desmond finished his beer and placed the empty bottle on the floor.

"Anyone wanna play spin the bottle?"

"What are you, twelve?" Steph asked.

Derrick laughed as Desmond spun the bottle. It spun, and spun, and spun, and it stopped on me. Desmond looked me in the eyes, made a smoochie face, then laughed. I didn't find it funny.

"You take the first spin, Adrian." I had no intention of kissing anyone in that basement, but I grabbed the bottle anyways, and it spun. My heart raced because I wasn't quite sure where it would land, so I closed my eyes until I heard, "Well, this is a bit awkward," from a voice I recognized.

I opened my eyes and the bottle was aimed toward Mel.

"That's unexpected." Desmond laughed. "Well, are you

guys going to kiss?"

"How about asking me if I want to kiss anyone?" Mel said.

"You're right. Do you want to kiss him?" Desmond replied.

A silence followed. "Just kiss him!" Desmond commanded.

Mel just looked at me for a few moments. I didn't know what to do, or what to say, so I just sat there, frozen.

"Can we put on a movie?" Mel asked.

"Yeah, sure. We can do that." Desmond grabbed his remote and showed us a selection of films we could watch. What had happened had made me feel very weird. But I think what made me feel most weird about it was thinking about how Desmond just assumed that it was okay for me to kiss Mel, and how I didn't say anything about it.

Mel picked the film. It was a documentary about climate change, but as the film began, I laid back in the La-Z-Boy, shut my eyes, and before long, I was asleep.

I didn't even remember dreaming about anything, but I woke up to voices.

"I think you're really great. I've thought so for a while. What's stopping you?"

"I want to, but he's right there," I heard.

"He's sleeping."

"I know, but what if he wakes up?"

My eyelids opened a tiny crack. I could see Steph and Derrick both asleep in their chairs, but my eyelids were so heavy that they closed again. But I kept listening.

"He won't."

I heard a giggle. I heard another giggle. A familiar giggle.

"Then get closer, cute boy." Then the smooching noises filled my ears not long after. Something in my stomach twisted. It was jealousy, disappointment, and anger. I sat up to see Mel and Desmond making out. I saw the way she played with his hair, and the way he held on to her shoulders, and the way they both seemed so . . . happy. It all sunk in, filling my chest, causing my heart to drop. Then Mel noticed me from the corner of her eye. She pulled away and shortly after, Desmond turned his head in my direction. Silence filled the air, and I kept my head down. I loved her, but she liked someone else, and that someone wasn't me.

"Dude, if this is weird then maybe . . ." Mel began.

"This is weird. I don't like this. I don't like him. I don't want to be here," I said in a low voice. "Why did you invite me?"

"Because I wanted you to get out of your house. Outside of your head."

"Well maybe my head is the only place where I don't get hurt."

Mel sat in silence.

"Come on, man. Don't be like this. She can kiss whoever she wants," Desmond said.

"That's not what you implied earlier, asshole," I snarled.

Desmond cocked his head back. He didn't like being called an asshole. Then he turned to Mel.

"It was just a joke, right, Mel?"

"It wasn't a funny one," she replied with her head down.

"Okay, I'm sorry. God, I can't even joke about anything anymore with you social justice warriors. If you guys don't want to be here, then maybe you should both leave."

Mel's eyes darted to Desmond, and I could see her frustration and disgust.

"You know what? I thought there was more under your macho man, preppy art student persona. Desmond, you're so fake."

"Yeah, and right now I'm going to be real. If you don't like my hospitality then get out, both of you. Take your drama elsewhere."

I stormed out of Desmond's house. When I opened the front door I let Mel exit first, then I slammed that door as loud as I could, hoping it woke up his parents. I checked my phone and it was shortly after three in the morning. Mel looked hurt and confused, just like me.

"Can you walk me back to my car?" she asked quietly.

I wanted to say no, but I didn't. We didn't say a word to each other while walking back to Dreamer's Corner. I was angry, but also sad. I was angry because I felt betrayed, but I was sad that she liked someone else, and I'm sure she knew. As much as it hurt, I still cared about Mel. I knew that she still cared about me, but not in the way I cared about her. That was the weird part, realizing that maybe our heartbeats weren't on the same wavelength, and I didn't know how that made me feel. She lit a cigarette on the way back. I could tell that the whole situation put her on edge.

I was fatigued and out of breath. I just wanted to be home and in my bed, but I fought through it. Mel could tell I was tired and tried to give me a hand, but I swiped my arm away. I didn't see her reaction, but I heard a big exhale from her direction.

It was a quarter after three, and we were back at Dreamer's Corner. Mel's car was still there, and she unlocked the doors while taking puffs.

"Do you need a lift?" That was the only thing she had said to me since we left Desmond's place. Her eyes told me that she wanted me close, but at that moment I needed distance more than I needed her.

"I think I need space," I said.

"Oh," she replied, her shoulders dropping. She began taking deep breaths and tried to readjust herself. I knew she was using all her strength to do so — she was never one to let me see her be weak. She wasn't weak. It was just a difficult situation for both of us.

I didn't know what to say, so I just stood there soaking in the awkwardness. She lit another cigarette, no doubt hoping it could ease her emotions, but it only created more smoke. Eventually, I walked away. Not long after, I heard her car engine turn on and saw her drive off. I hoped distance would do me well because that punk show hadn't.

# CHAPTER 13
# Don't Bite the Hand

I thought that time and distance would put my emotions at ease, but a week later I was still as hurt as I was that night. The way they both kissed, and knowing that she had moved on. I was angry. I was angry at Mel. I was angry at Desmond. He was such a jerk. I couldn't believe the way that he kicked Mel out of his house at three in the morning. Nothing about that night sat well with me. I met up with Donny at school that day and we chilled during the lunch hour.

"Ever think of getting a dating app?" Donny asked me while leaning against a locker and swiping through his phone.

"That thought never occurred to me," I said honestly.

"Well, you have to be eighteen to get on most of them, according to the app shop."

"Well I guess that solves that problem."

"Not if you lie, genius. Get one, and you'll get over Mel fast."

Donny really didn't understand how relationships worked. I didn't just want to be with someone for the sake of being with them. That felt wrong and like a waste of time. Relationships are something meant to grow and flourish, not some band-aid solution for the emptiness I was feeling.

"I don't think I want that right now," I said. "But thanks anyways."

"To each their own." Donny shrugged, eyes still dedicated to his phone.

A numbness had settled inside me. It was pretty much the only feeling I knew anymore. I was empty. I had emptied my fat into toilet bowls, I betrayed love for fantasies of being fit. I opened my eyes to heartache and then I let my jealousy transform into something toxic. That was why my tank was empty. I was fighting off tears in that moment, so I left school early. I went home and darted straight to the kitchen. I ate two peanut butter sandwiches, a bowl of ice cream, and a chocolate bar. I had to fill myself with something. I ate, and I ate, and I ate, hoping it would numb the pain. Afterward, I felt even worse. Once I got to my room, I let myself cry, hoping it would wash away the heartache.

Later on that evening, I dragged myself out of bed and into the bathroom. I undressed and put each foot on the scale. The zeros flashed on the screen, and then I saw 188. That was three pounds heavier than I had been recently. I cringed because I knew it meant I had to purge. I was so mad at myself for letting a scale control me.

If I hadn't started purging, I'd probably still be with Mel. But I just wanted to look and feel normal, and there was always a cost. I got on my knees in front of the toilet seat and did what I had to.

Afterward I sat leaning against the door. It was shortly after three in the afternoon and I heard my cell phone begin to ring. I ignored it. It rang again. I ignored it. It rang again, and finally I grabbed it furiously, answering with, "What!?"

"Hey, man," I heard from the other end. It was Mel's voice. "I thought . . . maybe we could talk. Can I pick you up, or something? Do you wanna come to my place?"

"I can just meet you there," I said without thinking. Maybe it was a stupid idea, but maybe I could get some clarity and take away some of the pain. I got up, brushed my teeth, and chewed some gum to get rid of the smell of vomit, then made my way to Mel's.

During the walk there my mind was flooded with feelings of relief and distress. I was relieved because she wanted to see me, but I was very upset at everything that had happened — her leaving me because of my eating disorder, her making out with Desmond, and her still pretending to care. It was a chilly journey there, but I saw her basement light on. I didn't bother going to knock on her front door. By the time I got to the back door, she was already waiting.

"Hey, come in." She opened the door wider.

Her room was the same. It was very neat. It had more band posters than before, but it had been a while since I was there. She sat down on her bed, palms in her lap, while I pulled up a chair. We sat in silence for a few moments. Then she just spoke.

"Hey, Adrian. I'm sorry. The concert was a bad idea."

"It was."

"I think we need to talk . . . about a lot of things."

"I think so, too." I was a bit blunt.

"Listen, Desmond and I kinda had a small fling for a bit. I thought he was nice, but it was all an act. He's not a nice guy."

"You don't think?"

Mel let out a breath. "Listen, you don't have to be an asshole right now."

She was right. I didn't have to be rude to her. But I wanted to be.

"I thought . . . I thought I should have tried to get you out of the house at the time. Desmond didn't care that you were my ex. He doesn't get bent out of shape over stuff like that," she continued. "It was dumb, and I don't know what else to say, besides sorry. You didn't deserve that."

I let that sink in for a moment, but it didn't put me at ease. There was still a lot more that bugged me.

"I didn't realize how much of a jerk he was. He just assumed I would take his side, even when he did something wrong. Thank you for calling him out on the spin the bottle thing. That was weird."

"I should have said something sooner. He's in your class, isn't he?"

"He is. He's just been pretending that I don't exist. Typical boys."

She let out another breath and curled up, propping her head on her knees. She was hurt, and so was I. I still needed answers though. I figured it might be the only time I could ask. I thought back to months before on our "cheat day" and why she left me. I was left with so much hurt and confusion that it was almost impossible not to wonder what her real intentions were that night.

"Why did you leave?" I asked.

"What do you mean?"

"That night, well, morning. I mean, when you found me throwing up."

She looked up at me and let out yet another breath. There was a story in her, one that would reveal something, and I wanted to know what it was.

"There's a lot behind it."

"I have time," I said.

"Fine." She shook her head and stood up. "When I saw you that night, I just didn't wake up and decide to leave you that morning. There was more —" She paused abruptly. I knew that it was going to be hard, but I wasn't sure to what degree. I got as settled in as I could. This was strange territory for both of us.

"Listen, when I saw you purging, it made me feel really unsafe."

I was confused. "Why did it make you feel unsafe?"

"You don't know this, but two years ago, I had an eating disorder. It was bad. Hospitalization bad." I hadn't known about any of that. A wave of emotions hit me hard, and I wasn't sure how to sort them out. I had no idea what to say, but it also gave me a piece of this weird puzzle I was attempting to solve.

"I didn't know," was all I said.

"At my lowest, I was at ninety pounds. Dude, I was sick.

They kept me in the hospital for a month and then I was put in a treatment program that lasted from then until last February. I only finished the program a year ago," she confessed. Mel took another deep breath. She'd been holding in a lot and now she was letting it all out. "When my parents divorced I stayed with my dad. He wasn't making much money at his shop, so he couldn't afford to keep me in karate. I was depressed. I'd lost my mom, my community, and I felt alone. I found comfort in food and began gaining weight, and he noticed. My own father called me fat and so did kids at school. It got to me . . . it weighed on me. I felt so gross in my own body. I was tormented about it in my own home, at school — I had no safe space. I felt like I had to change to be loved, so I did what you did, and I couldn't stop." She continued after a breath. "Everyone would compliment my appearance when I began losing weight — my dad, people I went to school with. I liked it for a bit, then I resented it. But I couldn't stop. One day at my dad's shop, I just fainted and hit my head . . . hard. My dad called an ambulance, and that's how he found out." I hadn't known about any of that. I wasn't sure what or how to feel about it.

"I got lucky that I made it past that point in my life. I don't tell anybody about it, but I've told you. Through that treatment program, I learned to care about my body a different way, through exercise, healthy diets, and self-care," she explained.

Melody had seemed like the type of person who had herself together, but she really put herself out there for me to see.

"I had no idea," I eventually said.

"No, no, you didn't. Adrian, when I saw you that night,

throwing up, sticking your fingers down your throat, it brought me back to a place where I couldn't be. I felt really lost, like I didn't know you. I thought I had been helping you lose weight on a healthy track for months, and seeing you do that, well, it just felt like I'd been betrayed and that my worst fears were involved with the same person as I was."

She paused for a moment and put her face in her lap. When she brought her face back up, it was covered in tears.

"I saw the things I was running away from: my fear, my insecurities, my past, my trauma. I saw it wrapped around the boy I loved. It hurt, and it scared the hell out of me. I had to leave."

More tears began rolling down her cheeks, but she didn't make any noise. I didn't know how to feel, or how to react. It put the puzzle pieces together, but it didn't quite cool down the hurt that I felt. Why hadn't she been open about it in the first place? I felt like I was left in the dark, and it wasn't a good feeling. She could have told me, and it could have helped put things into context earlier. If she went through the same thing, and if she would have told me her story, it could have been avoided. I went on the offensive.

"Mel, that's . . . Why didn't you tell me this before? I was in the same position that you were in."

"Because it freaked me out, dude. I don't think you understand —"

"If *you* had understood, you wouldn't have left me like that. I needed help and support. I needed someone and you left me there."

"Adrian, that wasn't my intention —"

I cut her off. "But that's what you did. Maybe if you had kept close, then I would have lost weight at a healthier rate, maybe I wouldn't have this stupid excess skin, maybe I wouldn't have to wear layers, maybe I wouldn't be drowning in depression." God, I was pissed off.

"I'm sorry, I didn't know what to do. I was spooked, okay?" she said defensively.

"Yeah, jump scares or horror movies don't scare you. But people who need help do."

"I'm sorry!" she cried. "I still care about you —"

"If you cared about me, then I wouldn't have ended up doing what you already did," I growled.

That hurt her. I immediately regretted saying it. Mel's eyes widened, not expecting that kind of anger from me. All my feelings had grown into something else, and that something was hurtful, spiteful, and full of misplaced fury, but aimed toward someone who didn't deserve any of it. There was a long silence. It was uncomfortable, but she didn't weep. She just sat there with her head down.

I wanted to say sorry, but my ego wouldn't let me. I put my jacket on to leave.

"So, I guess this is kinda it, isn't it?" she asked.

"You already made that choice," I replied.

She wasn't fighting back the tears — they were already rolling down her face. She inhaled heavily and exhaled so much sadness. So I left her alone to wallow in it. I shut the door on my way out, zipped up my jacket, and made my way back to my room, knowing I'd hurt the one I loved most. Deep down I really wished I hadn't said any of it.

# CHAPTER 14
# Disparity

I didn't get much sleep that night. My parents got in late, and that morning my mom saw me walk to the bathroom.

"Are you going to school?" she asked.

"I have a free first period," I lied. I wasn't going to school that day. I decided as soon as I stepped out of bed. Though if I told her I had a free period, then she'd leave the house for work before I would have to be out.

"All right, babes. Have a good day. I'll see you this evening."

"Later, Mom," I replied.

My dad had already left earlier that morning, so after I heard my mom shut the front door I grabbed the scale and took off all my clothes again. I stepped on it to see the zeros doing their thing, and it landed on 185. Back to where I was. I guess that was okay. I made my way downstairs and ate half a banana, a slice of bread, and a spoon of peanut butter. I didn't feel like eating very much.

After the night before, I knew I had to relieve a lot of stress, so I put on my runners and decided to go for a jog. I wasn't as embarrassed to jog now, especially during the day. If I wore layers, then I looked just like anyone else. I was wearing an all-black tracksuit as I ran down past Dreamer's Corner and made my way toward the mall. It was super chilly, and I was running out of breath really fast. It didn't take me long to realize that I didn't want to jog that day. I didn't want to do anything. I sat down on a bench and put my head in my hands, feeling sorry for myself. *I shouldn't have said any of that to Mel. She didn't deserve it.*

Suddenly, I heard a car pull up, followed by a honking horn. It startled me so much that I fell back off the bench.

"Earth to Adrian! Get in the car. You must be freezing." I knew that voice. I got to my feet and there was Scarlett waving for me to get in. I got in into her car, and the first thing she said was, "What are you thinking? You're in a tracksuit . . . jogging? It's freezing!"

"It's not that cold out."

"Young people are weird. It's *cold* outside."

She made her way onto the road and through the intersection.

"So, you fell off the face of the Earth. Looks like you made it back with a whole lot less of you."

"Oh, yeah, uh . . . Thanks."

We approached a red light and began to slow down.

"What happened to you, man? Not a text? Not a hello?

Not a 'I'm doing okay but I've moved on from King's'?"

That was valid. After Mel left me, that was the end of King's for me. I hadn't even told Scarlett or Ryan that I wasn't coming back.

"I've had a lot going on." I didn't know what else to say.

"Seems like it. Do you still talk to Mel? She stopped going shortly after you did. But she at least thanked us for helping her out."

Yeah, I'd kind of just ghosted everyone at King's. It wasn't a good plan, but I seemed to be a body of bad decisions.

"Anyways, I just got off from working my night shift. Seems like you're skipping school. Wanna grab a coffee?"

"Sure," I replied. I didn't drink coffee, but I did want to catch up.

Scarlett drove into the drive-thru, bought herself a small black. She had a feeling I'd only like my coffee if it had a lot of milk and sugar, so she ordered me a double-double. She was right. She paid the employee and handed me my coffee.

"Warm up, kid. My heater isn't working."

The coffee was hot, and I could feel it through the paper cup. She pulled over in the parking lot and sat back.

"So, what the hell happened? You left kickboxing, but you lost the weight. What did you do?"

I didn't want to tell her. I knew she'd be ashamed of me if I did. I valued Scarlett's opinion even if I hadn't kept in touch. I hadn't planned to fall out of touch, it just kind of happened. I would have reached out to her eventually, but I just didn't know when. So much had happened since I had last seen her. I trusted her, and I felt like I was carrying a weight in my heart made of pain, anger, and regret. It all just kind of flowed from there. So I poured everything out.

I told Scarlett that I had started purging and about the night that Mel had found me over the toilet. I told her that Mel had left me. I told her that I began purging more and more, I told her about my excess skin, I told her about my doctor's appointment, I told her about Mel coming to get me from the hospital washroom. I told her about that night at the punk show, I told her about waking up to see Desmond and Mel kissing, I told her about needing distance, and finally, I told her about the night before. I told her about Mel revealing her past to me. And how I had unloaded all of my anger onto Mel right after. It was a lot. It was a long story, but Scarlett listened. I could see her face go from worried, sympathetic, shocked, and then mad.

"That's a lot, kid," was all she said, and then she took a long sip of her drink. "You're lucky I have coffee. Because you just unloaded a lot of bullshit on me."

*Bullshit?* I was a bit confused. I was being honest. I'd just poured my heart out to Scarlett, and she threw it back in my face.

"I'm sorry, you've been through a lot. It seems as though you're carrying a lot of anger because of it. Reasonably so," she told me. "Though, when you carry so much anger, it can often be misplaced. Mel only wanted to help you."

"Then why did she leave me when she found me purging?"

"Can you maybe think for a second?"

"What do you mean?" I asked.

"Maybe this isn't all about you. Mel was going through

153

her own stuff, too. Sometimes, you have to look out for yourself. That's what she did in that moment. You told me that she suffered from an eating disorder, and she saw you suffering from one, too. Maybe it brought back too many difficult memories? All the help she gave you was out of the kindness of her heart. She didn't owe you anything."

I didn't know why, but that put me on the defensive really quick. I didn't have a comeback, so I sat with those thoughts.

"She's given you so much of herself, and helped you so much, and that's how you act? That's very childish."

I didn't like being called childish.

"I'm not a child. I was hurt."

"Yes, but your hurt doesn't give you a right to treat the people in your life badly. That's just you being selfish."

That angered me, too. I wasn't selfish.

"What she did, that night, when she found me in the bathroom, Scarlett, that hurt me," I said, struggling to form the words as I began breathing heavily. It was difficult to stay calm. Scarlett made it seem like my hurt wasn't a big deal.

"I'm not saying she didn't hurt you, Adrian." Scarlett put a hand on my shoulder. "But sometimes you have to understand that hurt people, hurt people. It can be unintentional."

*Hurt people, hurt people?* That wasn't a concept that I'd heard before. I knew Mel was hurt, and I knew what I said wasn't right, knowing that made me feel a sudden surge of regret. I shouldn't have unloaded on Mel. She hadn't deserved that. She hadn't deserved any of that. But I'd done it anyway. It was immature, stupid, and shortsighted. Scarlett was right, about all of it.

My realization must have shown on my face because Scarlett smirked. "I think what you're feeling is called empathy. You should use it more. It can help you avoid situations like this one."

Scarlett was smug, but wise. I appreciated it sometimes. Other times it felt like kicking sand in a wound.

"I missed you," I said.

"I missed you, too, kid." She smiled. "Don't do your disappearing act on me again. There are people who care about you, y'know?"

"I know."

Scarlett drove me home, and I let everything sink in once more. At that point, I really regretted what I'd said to Mel. It wasn't fair. I didn't know what to do, so I kept my distance for a few weeks. I began reflecting a lot more. I thought about how much she had helped me along the journey. She'd tried her hardest. She put in so much work and asked for nothing in return. God, I was an idiot. I had a lot to own up to.

# CHAPTER 15
# *Inspiration*

*Scale, scale on the floor, do I weigh less than I did within the last twenty-four hours?* I thought as I stood on the scale a few weeks later and watched the display. Three zeros flashed and flashed until it read 178. Less than before. In my mind I thought it was a good thing. Standing shirtless and seeing myself in the mirror still made me feel uneasy. I watched my skin pour down around me as I met my reflection. Looking in the mirror became a difficult chore.

I ended up going to school that day and got the same old stares as I had before. Everyone wanted to know my secret, but it was a secret I wasn't proud of. I avoided eating breakfast that morning, some days I had very little, others I didn't have anything at all. Navigating through class was difficult because of it. How could I listen to Mrs. Thompson educate me about Canadian history if the rumbling inside of my stomach was the centre of my attention? My skin was dry, my eyes were heavy, so I rested my head on my desk. Before long I woke up to: "Mr. Carter! You seem to be in a different world. Anything on your mind?" Mrs. Thompson said in front of the class.

Honestly, food. I wanted to eat, but I didn't want to let myself.

"I didn't sleep very much last night," I lied. The truth was, I'd barely made it to school without fainting.

"A boy your age should get eight hours of sleep a night. Go get some water and come back when you're ready."

I went to the fountain and filled myself up. The water tasted better than it should have and I wanted every last drop. When I lifted my head, I saw a group of guys walk by. They were all huge and on the football team.

"Look at the MVP, Adrian Carter! I see you're putting in work at the gym," one of them said.

"Get it, bro," another told me.

As they passed, they all gave me pats on the back and a thumbs-up. Each pat felt like it was going to knock me over, but I forced a smile. I didn't like being complimented because of my appearance anymore. It felt really degrading, and I didn't know how to tell people that.

Back in class, I tried to focus, but I couldn't. I watched the clock and lunch was in twenty minutes. I was going to allow myself to have a granola bar to get myself through the day. It was just a waiting game. Out of nowhere I was hit in the head with a ball of paper. Mrs. Thompson didn't see, or she would have stopped class to find out who did it. I opened it up and it read: *Hey! Can you tell me your secret?*

*You look great, and honestly, you're really cute now.*

I looked back and saw Olivia smiling at me. I had known her since grade seven. She didn't want to know my secret, and I found the note a little bit insulting. I didn't find myself desirable when I was bigger either, but some things you should keep to yourself. I shook my head at her, and her smile faded into a frown.

When the lunch bell rang, I grabbed a granola bar from the cafeteria and one of the lunch ladies told me, "You're looking really healthy, kid. Your parents must be proud."

They were. My parents showed me off every time company came over, and I hated it. Guests didn't have to see me while I was smaller to appreciate me. I didn't feel any different and being desirable all of a sudden was extremely hurtful. I hated all of it.

I bought my granola bar and went up to the second floor to sit against the lockers. I didn't know where Donny was, but I kind of wanted to be alone. Though the loneliness didn't last for long. A student who I'd seen around a few times approached me. She was awkward, I was awkward. I couldn't tell if she was really awkward or just shy. She looked at me for a few more moments and finally spoke. "You're Adrian Carter, right?"

I nodded, my mouth still full of chewed-up granola bar.

"I know this is really weird. But I just wanted to tell you that you're a huge inspiration. Your transformation really motivated me to lose weight."

I paused while still chewing. I didn't know what to say, so I just stayed silent for a moment.

"Sorry, you're eating," she said. "I'm such a dork, but can

I show you what I looked like before?"

I swallowed my bar and said, "Hey. That's really cool. Yeah, sure."

She pulled out her phone, scrolled for a moment, and then passed it to me.

"See?" she said while showing me the photo. "I've lost twenty-seven pounds since September." You could see the difference in the photo. She went from being a bit on the chubby side to fit. She looked sad in her picture, but now, standing in front of me, she looked happy. She looked hopeful.

"Thank you for showing me that." I smiled. "I'm really proud of you. That's a huge accomplishment."

She blushed and told me, "Congrats on your accomplishment, too. You're really a huge inspiration — to a lot of people. My name is Kate."

"Nice to meet you, Kate." I extended a hand that she shook. She left after a moment, waving shyly.

Kate left me with a lot of thoughts. It was a lot to process that my weight-loss journey helped motivate others to begin theirs. I guess my transformation carried a lot of weight. No pun intended. But hearing that left me torn because how much damage did I have to do to my body to be called an inspiration? My secret was a double-edged sword. On the surface, I looked like an inspiration, but beneath it, I felt like a failure that hid mistakes in layers of clothes. Students often complimented my appearance. I didn't quite know how to take it, like that day in the cafeteria when I was swarmed. I felt so overwhelmed, but a lot of those students just wanted to tell me that they were proud of me. But would they say they were proud if they knew I purged? Would they say they were proud if they knew I wasn't eating often? I ate enough to make me not feel like I was about to pass out, but I didn't take proper care of myself.

As much as I could appreciate people supporting me, it didn't help. Maybe I was an inspiration to some, but only as far as their eyes could see. If they saw what was beneath my long sleeves, who knows what they would think of me. Would they still hold me in the same regard? Or would they say I needed help? They saw me as one thing, but I was a lot of things. Uneasy, unhappy, difficult, weird . . . but I think most of all, I was torn. I'd thought that losing weight would make life easier. I thought it would help me find love, happiness, and reassurance, knowing that I didn't have to feel insecure about my looks. But when I had to see my excess skin every day, I felt awful to the point of pushing everyone away. I felt alone, stranded, and trapped in a storm that I had created. I looked like a monster, so I guess I had to isolate myself like one.

# CHAPTER 16

# Her Left Hook

I couldn't find Donny anywhere that afternoon, and I didn't want to be alone. I sent him a text.

**Me:** Yoo, where you at?

There was no reply, and my battery was at eight per cent. I wandered the halls, hoping maybe his phone had died and that he was just chilling somewhere else. I thought about going to the library to see if he was there, then realized Donny was far too loud and talkative to last long in there.

I made my way to the cafeteria, and through the crowds of students, I saw Desmond in the distance, sitting at a table with two girls. I couldn't make out what he was saying, but he made them laugh, and he smiled, clearly enjoying the attention. He had gotten over Mel fast. He spotted me and gave me a subtle smirk. I returned the gesture with a middle finger, and wiped the smirk right off his face. I wasn't in the mood for his bullshit that day, or ever. I ended up hanging out by myself underneath a stairwell until the class bell rang.

There was a lot to think about under that stairwell. I had to make things right with Mel. She'd poured herself out to me, and I'd thrown it back in her face. Sure, I was mad. But it wasn't an excuse to treat people like crap. Mel deserved to be treated better. I opened up a journal from my backpack and began writing things that I could say to her.

*Hey, listen. What I said a few weeks back? It was dumb.*

*Hey Mel. I'm real sorry. That was stupid, and I wasn't thinking.*

*Mel, I don't know what to say other than I was wrong.*

None of it really stood out, and it made me frustrated. I needed to be authentic, I needed to be honest, I needed to be real. I had to let her know I was sorry, but not in a way that swept what happened under the rug. I had to be better.

I had no idea when I'd see Mel. I hadn't reached out to her at all. But in time I knew I would, so I sat there for my entire lunch hour, trying to write out what I wanted to say and how I wanted to say it. I felt like I was going in circles, getting lost somewhere in my words, in my own mind. Then the bell rang. I had English that afternoon on the third floor. I made my way up the stairs, and as I walked up there, I felt someone snatch the notebook. I looked back and saw Desmond. He ran back down the stairwell without saying a word.

"What the hell!?" I said. I ran back down the already crowded staircase, following him. He made his way through the entrance of the school right in front of the fountain. He knew there would be a crowd, and I should have known better.

"Come get it, loser." He held it in the air. I made my way toward him and mentally blocked out everyone standing around outside. Desmond was about to get a piece of me. I went to grab my notebook back, then out of nowhere I felt someone push me to the ground. Hard.

"Think you can just give my boy the finger?" I heard. Lewis. I got back to my feet as fast as I could, but he already had his grip on my collar and forcefully pinned me against the wall.

"Who do you think you are?" he barked. "You go in his home, start shit with his girl, then give him the finger?"

*Ha. His girl?* Mel wasn't property, and I doubt she wanted to be anywhere near Desmond after that. I knew better than to bite, so I stayed quiet.

"Got anything to say, lipo?"

I wasn't in the mood. First Lewis called me fatass and now he decided to call me lipo? I couldn't win.

"What's in the journal?" Lewis sneered.

"Don't," I said, scowling.

"There we go, now we got a reaction."

A crowd of students started forming.

"What are you guys? Some band of shitty supervillains?" a random voice in the crowd said.

"Shut up, idiot," Desmond snapped.

"Go back to private school, you pretentious asshole,"

someone else yelled at Desmond. The entire crowd erupted into laughter while his face turned red. I began to laugh, too. Lewis noticed and slammed me against the wall, hard.

I tried to fight back, but Lewis was a lot stronger than I was. I didn't exactly eat my vegetables and knew I wasn't going to get out of this using strength. So I sucker punched him in the gut. He let out a weird noise and dropped me. I shoved him out of the way with the little strength I had and tore my notebook out of Desmond's hand. He looked frightened and unprepared to see me in his face.

"Uhhh. Hey man, be cool."

"Desmond, stay the hell away from me, and Mel —"

Before I could finish that sentence, I felt a shove from behind. I face-planted into the concrete, and my notebook went straight into the air. I looked up and saw it coming down as its shadow graced my face. Everything was in slow motion, but all in real time. I could see students pointing at the notebook, and at me.

"Watch out, it's airborne!" someone yelled.

Then I heard a splash.

"No," I said quietly. I got back to my feet, and there it was, sinking in the school fountain. All my ideas, thoughts, and what I was going to say to Mel were sinking to the bottom. Before I could even crawl to get it, I felt Lewis grab me by the collar again.

"Look what you did, loser. You just lost your book. Was it worth it? I hope it was, because right now you're about to go in there, too." Lewis dragged and shoved me against the fountain railing.

"Lewis, don't!" I pleaded. Lewis had one hand wrapped

around my neck and used his other hand to lift my feet.

"Yeah! Throw him in there!" Desmond cheered.

"Shit, shit, shit! Lewis, what are you doing!" I tried to fight him off. But he was a lot stronger than I was. At that point I was holding onto the rail and freaking out. I could see the water, and Lewis was only getting more forceful. I was mad, upset, and I was going to look weak in front of everyone. Again. I closed my eyes, wishing I was strong enough to put him on his ass. Then suddenly gravity brought me back down and terror was replaced by surprise.

"What the hell are you doing!?" Lewis yelled. I opened my eyes, and someone I couldn't quite see knocked Lewis to the ground. They were wearing a black hoodie. Lewis tried to get back to his feet, but that was a mistake. As he stood up, he was met face-first with a left hook that sent him back to the ground. Lewis went limp.

A collective "OHHHH" escaped the students standing around us.

The person in the hood looked over to Desmond. His jaw dropped. "Oh shit!" he squealed then ran off back into the school.

"Figures," the hooded person said. They turned around and the hood came down. I saw long, black hair, eyes that looked too tired for this shit, and a face that was fearless.

"Mel," I breathed.

"HA! Lewis just got knocked out by a girl!" I heard someone in the crowd say.

"Hey, what's all the ruckus out there!?" It was Mr. Stephens's voice. Everyone scattered and went in different directions. In the corner of my eye, I saw Lewis get up and limp away, dazed.

"Come with me," Mel said. She gave me a hand, and I wrapped mine around it. She pulled me up, and we ran away from that school like it was on fire. We ran from bullies, we ran from standards that were set too high, we ran from teachers who didn't understand us. We ran away from fears and anxieties and scripts that were written out for us. I didn't know where we were going, but when she held my hand, she held it tight.

# CHAPTER 17
# Redemption House

Mel and I ran three blocks away from the school. I had no intention of heading back to class that afternoon. It was way too warm, and someone might have snitched. I couldn't believe Lewis tried to throw me into the fountain. I couldn't believe Mel went full ninja and knocked him out with one punch. Mel was running faster than I was, and I was having trouble keeping up. My energy was low. That's what happens when all you've eaten is a granola bar.

"Can we talk?" I said while slowing down.

She stopped with her back turned to me. She'd let go of my hand after we lost sight of the school. I could see her fist still formed. She didn't have to help me back there at the school, but she did anyways.

"Hey, listen. Thank you for getting me out of there." I approached her. "How'd you know I was there?"

She turned and glared furiously at me. It almost looked as if she wanted to punch me in the mouth, too. In all fairness, I did deserve it.

"I know you're angry," I began. Mel had been more sad than angry when we'd last spoken. Though feelings sometimes took a while before they properly set in. I had a feeling this was the case.

I tried putting a hand on her shoulder, but she shrugged me away.

"I'm more than angry. You're an asshole, you know that, right?"

"I know," I said honestly. "Can we just . . . Can we just go somewhere and talk?"

"Redemption House is around the corner. Buying me coffee would be a start," she told me.

All right, it was a start. I bought her a coffee, and we sat on the top floor that overlooked the park beside our school. It was a nice view. Mel sat across from me, arms crossed, and looked uninterested in the coffee I had gotten her. Maybe it was a mind trick. Maybe she was pissed. Possibly both.

"So . . ." I began.

"So." Mel shot at me.

God, I'd known it was going to be a difficult conversation, but I had no idea that I would be having the conversation right then. I tried thinking back to all the things I had written in my notebook, but my brain seemed to erase it all.

"There's a lot to talk about," I said.

"Yeah, there is," she replied.

It wasn't going to be easy. I stirred my coffee thoughtfully. If I could have gone back in time and changed what I'd done and what I'd said, then I would have. But life isn't that easy. We have to own our mistakes because that's the only way to grow. It was the only way I would regain any type of trust from Mel. God, I was an idiot. Mel's trust was one of the most important things I'd had, and I just threw it all away. I was stupid, I was selfish, I was arrogant and self-centred. I made everything about me.

"Mel," I began. "I just want to be upfront with you here. I'm not here to beg for your forgiveness. I don't deserve it. I'm here to apologize."

She stayed silent and took a sip of her coffee.

"I messed up. Completely. When you saw me that night, I was . . . I didn't know what to think. The next morning when you left, I was scared, I was frightened — I didn't know what to do. I shouldn't have said what I said to you, Mel. I was scared because I was still trying to figure out how to navigate in this strange turn of events that I'm supposed to call a body. I was scared because I felt lost without you. Everything came crashing down at once, and I acted terribly. None of this is an excuse, because this is on me."

Mel shook her head.

"Don't ever put this on me again, Adrian. Listen, I understand that you were hurt. But if you ever speak to me like that again, I'll be a disappearing act. Got it?"

"Got it."

"Good." She took another sip of her coffee and sighed. "As strong as you think I am, I'm not invincible when it comes to being hurt. You said some pretty awful things that night. I know you were dealing with a lot, but that's not an excuse to take it out on me. I'm not someone you can just dump your emotions on. I'm better than that, and you know better."

"I know, and I'm sorry."

"Are you though?" she asked. "I'm not just a character in your story who can keep all of your emotional weight. I can't do all the work for you."

"I know," I told her. "You've given me so much of yourself, so much of your time and energy. It was wrong for me to ignore all of that."

"It was. What you said to me was hurtful, and honestly, I really don't know where this puts us. I made myself vulnerable to you and you pushed me away. It was really revealing."

I sat there, worried. I didn't know where it put us, either. Mel was one person I felt like I couldn't lose. I cared about her a lot, but I wasn't deserving of her. If she chose to move on without me, then it was something I'd have to deal with, even if it hurt. We sometimes hurt the ones we care about because we think they'll take it. Not Mel. She made it clear. I still loved her, though. That hadn't changed.

"I guess it puts us at a standstill," I managed to say. "You didn't do anything wrong. It's on me to change, it's on me to make the difference."

"Well, then," she said. "What are you going to do?"

"What I have to."

"Be more specific."

"I'm going to stop treating everyone as if they're only a character in my story and work on rebuilding your trust."

I knew I was young, and I knew love was a concept I was still trying to learn, but the way her magic filled my lungs, the way her wisdom turned to song in my ears, the way her presence built comfort, the way she skipped rocks across my ocean made me feel as though love wasn't a strong enough word. Sometimes songs lose their magic, but she never did. Maybe it wasn't what grown-ups called love, maybe it was better, maybe it was softer, maybe it was what I wanted. But Mel didn't owe me any of that, so I knew it was my job to try to put things back in order, on her terms.

"I can't expect you to forgive me here and now. That's something I have to work toward."

"There's a lot you have to work on," she said. "You're so obsessed with the idea of how much you weigh, you're getting smaller and smaller. You're going to hurt yourself, and you can't expect me to sit here and watch you fade to nothing. Look at you, you can barely sit up straight."

She was right — I was nearly slumped over in my chair. I'd had no energy to fight back when Lewis held me against the wall.

"We can work on it."

"No. There's no 'we can work on it.' We have to fix this here, and we have to make a plan now. My life was at risk when I was in your shoes, and you're starting to resemble the skeleton I was. Adrian, you have to promise me. If you want to move forward with being friends with me, or something more, we have to stop this. I showed up today — I showed up here — because I still care about you. Even if you're being an ass."

Mel meant so much to me, but my eating disorder was something I couldn't break. If I could have, I would have.

"I . . . I don't know how," I said honestly.

"I know. I know how hard it is, Adrian. But I need you to trust me on this. You are going to hurt yourself and everyone around you."

Mel had been in the same shoes that I was currently in; she knew exactly how I felt, but I could imagine why she kept those skeletons in her closet.

"My entire life, I've been made fun of. I've been ridiculed and shamed for being overweight. I don't want to go back to that." I began getting teary eyed.

"You won't go back to how you were, not if you're surrounded by the right folks. But you have to understand, right now you're blindly running away from a fire, and every step you take is bringing you closer to a cliff."

She was right. I couldn't keep putting my body through this. Mel told me her horror story, and I couldn't go from being an inspiration to a tragedy. Too many people were counting on me: Mel, Scarlett, Kate, Ryan, Donny, Mom, Dad. I couldn't let them down.

I could feel the fear creeping inside of my stomach. The oceans that kept me stranded began rocking me pretty rough. This was a storm I had to make it through; I looked Mel in eye and asked, "Where do we start?"

# CHAPTER 18

# Not a Punching Bag

The next day, I knew what I had to do, but I was scared. Mel told me to meet up with her after school. Going back to school that day made me nervous. There had been no sign of Lewis. He'd taken a shot to his ego, being beaten up by a girl in front of a crowd of students. I was sure there was a video of it somewhere. Kids filmed everything. It was the lunch hour, and I sat underneath the stairwell with Donny and Mel. I'd decided I should come clean to Donny. I told him I had an eating disorder, and I told him about the purging. He sat against the wall with a look of concern and confusion.

"Wow, Adrian. I honestly had no idea that's what you've been doing," Donny said.

"Yeah. Not a lot of people do."

"You need to take care of yourself, bro. For real."

"I know."

Telling Donny about my eating disorder was awkward at first. I thought that speaking to men about insecurities was weird, but it turned out not to be so bad.

"Is there anything I can do to help, Adrian? I'm here for you, man."

"Thanks, Donny. I'm still working on myself, but I'll let you know. I appreciate it."

"I'm sorry I wasn't there yesterday. My phone was dead."

"It's all good, man. We took care of it. Well, Mel took care of it."

I looked over to Mel. She grinned. Mel and Donny seemed to be polar opposites sometimes, but she knew I loved him like a brother. He *was* my brother, so it was time we learned to talk about the difficult things.

"Boys never like to talk about real stuff, but I'm glad you two just did," Mel said. "I hope you're ready for later, AC."

"What's going on later?" Donny asked.

Mel's grin turned devilish.

"We're causing anarchy and vandalism. We're going to write on the side of the school, 'LEWIS GOT BEAT UP BY A GIRL!' And tomorrow his fragile ego will have him falling apart before our very eyes."

Donny laughed. "There's no way you two dweebs are spray painting the side of the school. What are you really doing?"

"We're breaking my scale," I said. "It's time to let go of that stupid thing."

Donny's face lit up with excitement.

"After all you told me, that's the dopest shit ever, my dude."

He put his hand up and gave me props.

"You know, man, I know I'm not a very complimentary person, but I'm proud of you, Adrian. You made a huge transformation, bro. Not even just body wise. But you're more mature, and you're owning everything, even your mistakes. I'm proud to call you my friend. You're friggin' awesome, Adrian."

Donny wrapped himself around me in a huge hug. It threw me off because he usually wasn't very emotional, but I hugged him back. It was nice.

We'd been through a lot together. From learning how to bike, to him teaching me how to shave, and now this. I assumed when he heard about me having an eating disorder, he would have thought less of me. I thought he would think I was sick, or needed help, or that I would hurt his vibe. But he was worried, concerned, and most importantly, he cared about me and wanted me to move forward.

"I love you, Donny," I said.

"I love you, too, AC."

He let go of his bear hug grip and gave me a huge pat on the back.

"God, I'm proud of you. You're one of the strongest people I know."

I smiled. Mel and Donny had been right all along. I was strong in a different way.

"I don't know about you, Mel, but ever since AC told me that story, it got cool in here."

Mel burst out into laughter. I frowned but ended up cracking a smile. It was fitting.

The lunch bell rang and we all drifted separate ways.

After school, Mel met me at my locker.

"You still wanna do this?" she asked.

I didn't know if I really wanted to, but I knew I had to.

"Yeah. I'm ready."

"Good, let's go. I'm parked over at Redemption."

Mel and I made our way across the park outside of school. It was starting to get a lot warmer. Spring was here, but the layers I wore weren't going anywhere. From the distance I heard, "Yo, Adrian!"

I didn't know who it was and didn't feel like talking, so Mel and I ignored it. Then I heard it again.

"Adrian!"

The voice was louder and aggressive. I kept walking because I just wanted to go home and get the scale and be finished with all of it.

"Adrian, watch out!" Mel shouted. I turned around and was pushed to the ground. Lewis was standing over me.

"You piece of sh —" I cut him off by kneeing him in the crotch. It was the second time he'd attacked me from behind, so it was fair game.

I stood up. "Listen, Lewis. I had a long day yesterday, and today is going to be a tough one. I'm not in the mood for this."

That didn't stop him, though. He charged forward and threw a sucker punch that caught me off guard. He sent me back to the ground. A herd of students walking through the park caught sight of this and started forming another circle around us.

*Not again,* I thought.

Lewis stood over me with vengeance in his eyes. He

couldn't accept what had happened yesterday. He had to prove to everyone here that he was tougher than me.

"You think your girlfriend can stand up for you all the time?" he barked. "I'm putting you in your place. You don't mess with me, kid."

Mel ran over and shoved Lewis out of the way, and grabbed my hand to pull me up quickly.

"Mel, don't get involved. If I don't end this here, he's only going to get worse. I know you can take him, you're a friggin' black belt."

"I know you can take him, too. You know kickboxing, dude. Take the safety off."

I turned around and saw Lewis get back to his feet. He was pissed.

I always saw fighting and martial arts as something that could be fluid and beautiful. But actually fighting someone? That was terrifying. Fear weighed down my lungs, but I knew I had to be light on my feet. I kept my fists in the air.

"Fight me like a man!" Lewis yelled as he balanced himself. He focused on me, and a sneer curved across his chubby face when he saw my ready stance. "Fight me like that."

Students around us started chanting, "Fight! Fight! Fight!"

I hated having an audience for anything, but Lewis loved it. Maybe that gave him an advantage. He charged toward me, but I stepped out of his way. It pissed him off, so he ran at me again. This time I stepped out of the way and kicked the back of his leg, forcing him down on one knee.

"Stop fighting like —"

"Like what? Like I know how?" I punched him square in the face, and the crowd of students all made a collective "OHHH" sound. They never failed to break routine. I didn't know where my energy was coming from, but Lewis made me livid. I wasn't going to let him bully me anymore.

Lewis got back up with a look of fury on his face.

"You shouldn't have done that!" he yelled. He threw a punch and I dodged it. He threw another one, and I managed to get out of the way, barely.

"God, you're boring," I said.

"Shut up!" he yelled at me and charged. I stepped out of the way this time and managed to trip him. He fell flat on the ground.

"No, Lewis. *You* shut up. Why do you have to yell everything? You really are like a shitty supervillain. You're going to lose this, just like you lost yesterday, then you're going to try again, and again, and again, and you're going to lose again, and again, and again. You know why? Spoiler alert: Because you're the loser here. Not me."

The words dug deep — I intended them to. I didn't care if I hurt Lewis anymore. I was done pretending as if I wasn't allowed to throw insults at him. He was a bully, but I was no longer going to allow myself to be a victim. He was the reason why I turned to food for comfort; he was the reason why I couldn't feel comfortable in my body. I wasn't going to let him torment me anymore.

"I hate you," he said as he got up.

"I'm sure you do, and I hate you, too. So throw down, show me what you can do," I replied while pointing to the ground in front me. I was ready, I was angry, and I was not going to take any shit from that asshole anymore.

Lewis got up and ran toward me. He threw more punches, but I dodged and threw a left hook into his stomach, and a right hook to his jaw. They were both going to leave marks. I thought I was winning, I thought I was going to kick his ass in front of everyone — then I felt his head smash against mine.

"You head-butted him!? What a prick!" someone in the crowd yelled.

Everything was spinning, and I stepped back. That wasn't cool. Lewis charged me and threw me to the ground. He got on top of me and started punching wildly. I used my hands to cover my face, but I couldn't block everything. He landed hit after hit. It hurt, and I was scared. Everybody was watching, and I was getting beat up. I looked weak in front of everyone again. Some of these students saw me as strong, they saw me as a motivation and an inspiration. Not Lewis. He was trying to rip that apart, he was trying to take away everything I'd done just to put himself on a higher pedestal. It was time I kicked that damn pedestal from under his feet. He tried throwing another punch, but I dodged it, kneeing him in the crotch again. He yelped like a wild animal, then I punched him in his side, again and again, until I had enough momentum to push him off of me. I got back to my feet and threw a punch for every time he'd called me a fatass. I threw another punch for all the times he'd put his hands on me. I threw another for thinking he was better than me. And I threw one more for good measure, just to let him know that I wasn't weak. The crowd was cheering, I didn't like it, but they did it anyways.

"Stop!" he cried. "I give up!"

"Are you done?" I yelled.

"Yes! I give up!"

"Well I'm not done." I walked forward to him and grabbed his collar to bring him closer.

"Let go of me!" he pleaded.

"I am the bigger person," I growled. "You, though . . . You're weak and pathetic."

He had to know. "You're a shitty supervillain who can't accept defeat, the loser who will never win. You'll never get the better of me again, Lewis, because you can't. Because you are weak and maybe I am, too. But you prey on weakness to help fight your own insecurity, and I'm done being your punching bag. You're the reason why I spent so much of my life hating myself, and now I'm going to become better."

I pushed his face into the ground, and he didn't even bother to get up. He just stared at me, and I could see the look of defeat, fear, and anxiety forming on his face. Honestly, I didn't care. The crowd began cheering, but it wasn't a victory I wanted to celebrate. I was pretty upset at the whole thing, but Lewis needed to know I wouldn't let him treat me like that anymore. I was glad that it was finally over.

"You ready, now?" Mel put a hand on my shoulder.

"Yeah. I'm ready," I said.

# CHAPTER 19
# Weightless

"Are you okay after that?" Mel asked as she pulled out of the Redemption House parking lot.

"Yeah, I think so. He had to go down."

I was still thinking about what had happened back there. *I just beat up Lewis in front of everyone.* A part of me felt good, really good. Another part of me felt indifferent because I hadn't wanted to do that. But deep down, I knew it was necessary. Mel didn't like violence either, but she knew Lewis had to be put in his place.

"He's done, and we won't have to worry about him any longer," I reassured myself.

"You're right," Mel said. "So, to your place?"

"Yeah. To my place."

Mel parked outside of my house, and I told her to wait in the car. I would only be a minute. I went inside, avoided my parents, and darted straight to the bathroom to check my face. It was a bit red, but it didn't seem as if it would leave a mark. Lewis had gotten a few good licks in. My phone began buzzing. It was text messages from Donny.

> **Donny:** AC, WHAT HAPPENED!!?!? I heard you beat up Lewis!? Are you a superhero or something, homie?

I didn't feel like one. I texted him back.

> **Me:** It's true. Keep it on the DL though ☺
> **Donny:** Mannnnn!!!! You are the shit.

It was hard not to smile at that. I put my phone aside and looked across the bathroom at my scale.

Did I want to step on it one more time? Did I really want to break this thing? Was I ready to move on? Those questions circled within my head, and I couldn't really answer any of them. I looked at myself in the mirror and saw a lot less of me than I had months ago. But underneath it all, there was so much more. Within the past while, I had taken in so much: the good, the bad — everything. It all weighed on me. But I wasn't meant to carry the weight of everything. I couldn't continue to carry the insecurity or be locked away in the cage of my own self-harm. Mel was outside, and I was there, trying to find the strength inside of me to pick up that stupid scale and break the one thing that controlled me.

I went over to it and stuck one foot on it. The zeros flashed. I felt like I was lost at sea, and that the scale owned me. It made me afraid to eat, it made me starve myself, it made me scared to be confident in my own body. That scale made me afraid to see my own beauty.

I stepped off the scale before the flashing zeros gave me a number. I sat against the wall and looked at myself in the mirror. I looked tired, sad, and drained. But I also saw beautiful brown skin, I saw determination to change, I saw the strength to move on.

I was tired of it. I was tired of having to starve myself just to see a lower number, I was tired of not having energy, I was tired of being hungry, I was tired of hurting myself when I purged. It did me no good. It was time for me to reclaim my body.

"It's time to say goodbye," I said softly.

I knew that it wouldn't solve my eating disorder. There was still so much to do, so much to unlearn, so many bad habits to break. But it started with this. I put the scale in my backpack and left.

Mel honked her horn when she saw me.

"Thought you might have gotten cold feet," she said.

"I thought I would, too," I said, getting in.

"I'm glad that you didn't."

"Then we better break this thing before I do." I was half serious.

Mel put her foot on the gas and we drove off. I wasn't quite sure where we were going, or how we were going to break it. I didn't ask too many questions. She drove back to her place, and put her car in park.

"Well, do we have a plan to break this thing?" I asked.

"I didn't really think that far ahead. I have a car, and an eager foot to put on the gas." Mel grinned.

"I like your spirit." I smiled back.

"Do the honours of putting it in position?"

I took the scale out of my backpack and walked about forty feet away. I could hear Mel revving the car's engine.

This was it. It all started with stepping on a scale, and it was going to end with us breaking one.

I was afraid to let go. I wouldn't be able to check my weight as much as I had been. What if I gained weight? I couldn't go back to being as big as I was. I might have beaten up Lewis, but that dude left me with a lot of scars, and that was what led me to the scale in the first place. The scale kept me lost in a sea of uncertainty, so I had to remind myself that it was my body and I had to let myself feel free. It was time to let go.

"This is *my* body," I whispered to the scale I held in front of me.

"Are you ready!?" I heard Mel yell.

I looked at the scale one last time. I was really doing it. My heart began racing, and I knew that it was the catalyst. I knew that my body would be mine again. I knew it was time for change and I knew where to start. I dropped the scale to the ground and moved back as Mel hit the gas with the intention of turning my scale into nothing more than a bad memory. I watched as my heart raced and prepared myself to let go of my bad habits. It was time.

As Mel drove over the scale, I saw it smash into what seemed like hundreds of pieces. They all felt like pieces of me, the ones I had to let go of. All the small bits went flying in the air and came down. I covered my head so none of the pieces would fall in my hair, and watching that felt more validating than losing my last ten pounds. I no longer felt like I needed a number to tell me I was beautiful. I thought back to every moment I had taken off my clothes and stepped on it. I felt every moment of disappointment, frustration, regret, anger, uncertainty, and depression fade away as I heard Mel hit the brakes.

"Heck yeah!" she shouted.

She put the car in park and ran over to see the damage. She'd got it pretty good. It snapped into three big pieces. Screws and plastic were scattered everywhere.

"Well, how do you feel?" Mel asked.

"Like there's a weight off my shoulders."

Mel smiled at the pun. "Good." Then she wrapped me in a hug. I hugged her back.

I could see the screen of the scale over her shoulder. The three zeros flashing back and forth as if it was asking me: "How could you?"

*Just like that,* I thought, followed by a middle finger.

The zeros flashed into nothing, causing a part of my anxiety to dissolve. Not all of it, because there was still one more wrong I had to right.

"Mel," I spoke with my arms wrapped around her.

"Yeah?" she asked.

"Can we talk about . . . stuff?"

"Yeah," she whispered. "We can talk . . . about stuff."

She grabbed my hand, pulling me toward her car.

"Let's go somewhere else," she said, and we did.

We left the pieces of the scale lying there. She backed up over it, which made me laugh. She made me feel so many things, and I wanted to tell her everything. I knew that breaking the scale wouldn't fix everything, but it was a start. A pretty damn good one.

# CHAPTER 20
# Her Melody

We drove around the city for a while until Mel took an exit onto the highway. We left the city, and eventually we drove past grass, trees, and under a clear sky. I didn't ask where we were off to and she didn't say. There was so much I wanted to say and there was so much I wanted to apologize for. An apology wasn't going to make a difference, though. I had to put in the work, and I was determined to. She drove past a few small towns outside of Halifax.

"So . . . Mel," I began.

"Yeah?" she said looking pretty focused on the road.

"Where are we going?"

"To a happy place."

"Yeah, but where?

"Adrian . . . just enjoy the ride, okay?"

"Okay," I said.

She was pretty determined about it and I didn't want to ask too many questions.

We were driving for a couple of hours. I tried keeping myself busy, but I was so focused on the moment that I was anxious for the entire ride. Eventually Mel turned onto a dirt road and floored the gas, causing me to sink in my seat.

"Sorry," she said. "I have to floor it here so we don't get stuck."

As she drove down the dirt road, we were surrounded by trees. The leaves were growing back, and some of the branches were swiping against the car.

"I hope they don't leave scratches," I said with concern.

"It'll be fine." She smiled.

I trusted her, but I had to work hard to get her to trust me again.

She parked her car down the road in front of what looked like a camping ground. The sun was beginning to die down, and the birds were beginning to fly home to the east coast again. It was warm. It was spring.

Mel ripped the keys out of the car, opened the door, and said, "Wanna go for a hike?"

I didn't really have a choice in the matter. So I said, "Yeah, let's do it." I wasn't exactly sure what I had gotten myself into.

Mel popped opened the trunk and grabbed a pair of heavy-duty boots and a backpack.

"Sorry, I would have asked you to bring yours if you have any, but this was kind of a spur of the moment decision."

"It's all good." I shrugged. My sneakers were eventually going to bite the dust, though this hiking trip might bring them closer to it faster.

"Follow me," she said as she began walking down a path. I obeyed. I was hours away from the city, in an environment I wasn't exactly used to, and pretty sure I had seen a sign that said, "BEWARE OF BEARS" — although my imagination might have made that up. I had all the trust in the world for Mel. I still loved her, and I wanted her to stay close. That was what I wanted to talk about. But I was scared. Mel didn't have a reason to love me back. I'd put her through a lot, and I shouldn't have. But she was still there, and maybe that counted for something?

We made our way to a wide river with a fallen tree lying over top of it.

"How fearless are you feeling this evening?" Mel asked with a grin.

"What? You can't be serious. No."

"What's stopping you? You just beat up a bully and helped destroy your parents' property. You can't walk over a little tree?"

"Oh, Mel. I've already been enough of a badass today."

"No, you haven't. Come on, take my hand." She extended her hand to me.

She wasn't going to stop until I did what she wanted. I sighed, and gave her my hand.

"Go slow," she said softly. "Don't pay attention to the water, just focus on me."

We made our way on top of the tree, and we slowly stepped across. I could feel fear creep into the back of my head.

"Don't feed the fear." She'd read my mind.

"I'm trying not to."

We were halfway across before I looked at the water, it was deep.

"Oh, man." I began to freak out and lost my balance. I almost fell backward into the water, but Mel was stronger than I gave her credit for. She yanked me back onto the tree.

"Be cool," she said. "Regain your balance, pay the water no mind."

So I tried, and we made our way across, one step at a time, together.

"See, look, we're almost there. Jump!"

Mel let go of my hand and jumped down onto the muddy ground. I had nothing to lose, so I jumped, too. I landed ankle-deep in mud.

"Okay, maybe we should have gotten you boots," Mel said apologetically.

"Maybe." I lifted one mud-soaked shoe to see. We both broke out into laughter.

"Come on." She grabbed my hand again. "Just a bit further."

Mel pulled me out of the mud and onto a path. The path led up a hill that oversaw nothing but a clear sky. I was out of breath and low on energy.

"Eat this." Mel smiled as she pulled an apple out from her backpack. I took a bite, and it was good. Maybe eating wasn't so bad. I wanted to do that more.

Mel tightened her grip on my hand to help me. We made it to the top of the hill as the sun went down. Night began to fill the air as I was catching my breath. "Why did you bring me out here?" I asked.

"The place should be close by," she said while gazing into the distance. She looked anxious and worried.

"There!" She pointed.

Down the hill, a short distance away, there was a small cabin with a fire pit just off of a lake.

"There it is." Mel had a smile that was fuelled by nostalgia.

We made our way down the hill toward the cabin. There was a sign that said, "PROPERTY OF MARTIN WOODS."

Mel rolled her eyes at it.

"Is this the place you told me about that night we sat on the roof of the school?" I began putting the pieces together.

"Yeah. Yeah it is," she replied.

It was beautiful. The cabin was still in great shape, although Mel told me she hadn't been there since she was a kid. There was chopped up firewood at the side of the cabin, and Mel threw some pieces into the fire pit.

"Let's set it ablaze in a bit. I wanna show you something," she said.

Mel brought me over to the lake. The night sky reflected on it like a mirror.

"When I was a kid, my mom told me that I was magic because I could skip rocks across the stars," she recalled as she threw rocks that bounced on the lake.

"I don't feel so magic lately. I feel really alone. I feel like a lot of people hurt me, intentionally or not. It really sticks with you. But this place, it reminds me of happy. Well, at least the formula to happy."

"So what is the formula to happiness?" I asked.

"It's a mixture of sorts. Maybe it's looking at ourselves in the mirror and thinking, 'holy shit I'm resilient.' But nobody builds resiliency from having a happy, easy life. It's always built upon a foundation of pain. Adrian, when I was in the hospital, I was in a lot of pain, but I'm still here. I survived, and I learned how to smile again. I learned how to have a good day, and dude, today was a good day. Today felt like the magic I'm always searching for. That's what I want to live for."

She skipped rocks across the lake with an unapologetic grin. "Try it." She passed me a rock.

I did, and the rock sank as soon as it hit the water.

She laughed. "There's still a lot to teach you, AC."

I just grinned. I didn't know what to say, because there was so much I wanted to tell her. So many feelings wrapped up in my chest. Instead of bringing them up, we skipped rocks for a bit, enjoying the quiet and being away from bullies, teachers, and parents.

I was one of the people who hurt her. I regretted it every day. We hurt the people we love because we because we think they can handle our pain, too. It's not our loved one's job to carry that burden, and Mel didn't owe me anything. It had taken a lot for me to realize that.

"Let's start that fire, eh? It's starting to get chilly," Mel said, and we walked back to the campsite.

"Give me your wallet." Mel had her hand out.

I passed her my wallet, and she grabbed the piece of paper that had her number on it and set it ablaze with her lighter, dropping it on the firewood. We sat down on an old wooden bench that was placed in front of the fire pit.

"You wanna spend the night here?" Mel asked, looking back at the cabin. "The nostalgia is giving me a throwback."

"It's Friday. Yeah, we can spend the night."

Mel smiled while warming up near the flames.

"So, you wanted to talk? About stuff?" she brought up.

My heart began sinking in what felt like quicksand, but I knew I had to be honest.

"Yeah," I began. "I . . . uh . . . I wanted to talk about stuff."

"What kind of stuff?"

"About you, and about me."

"Oh," she said, drifting off into what felt like anxiousness.

"Yeah," I said. I could feel it, too. "I . . . still have major feelings for you. You give still give me butterflies. I know this might be weird, I know this might be sudden."

"I could feel it coming." She looked up. "You haven't said much at all since we parked. Honestly, Adrian. You still give me butterflies, too. But this leads to the question, is this what we both need right now?"

That was a good question. Was it what I needed? Was it what she needed? I didn't know. What I needed was to find a support system to help me get back on track to health. Mel needed support, too. She needed healing, and maybe some space. The last few years hadn't exactly been easy for her.

"I don't completely know what you need right now," I began. "But all I can do is offer myself. I can offer my time and energy. Mel, you've given me a lot of kindness in the past months, and I had took advantage of it. I learned that the hard way. But this isn't all about me. This is about you, too. I don't want you to feel like you're not appreciated. Because I appreciate you so, so much."

"Thank you," she replied. "And I know. I know that you're sorry, I know you'll change. I wouldn't say that about many guys." She looked up at the stars, and maybe got lost in her thoughts. Maybe she thought about what she needed. I sat there looking at the stars, too, wishing I was somewhere in the spectrum of her desire. And honestly, I think that was the scariest part of it all. Mel was someone special, and I didn't want to lose her. The fire crackled as I watched her glow underneath the moonlight. She illuminated parts of me that I never knew existed. She brought out the best of me, and I hoped she knew that it had all started with her.

"I've been thinking about this a lot, too, Adrian." She took in a breath. "But I want to know how you're feeling. Where do you see yourself, fighting your problem? I don't want to add fuel to the fire."

"I don't know where I stand with it," I said honestly. "I'm scared. I'm scared about a lot. I'm scared that maybe Lewis might come back and try to fight me again, I'm scared that maybe I'll go and just buy another scale, and I'm scared that I'll have a future without you. I'm scared that I'll start purging again. But I think the only thing I can do is hold myself accountable for the actions that have put me here, and hold myself accountable for the mistakes I'll make in the future. There are going to be mistakes because I'm the furthest thing from perfect. I'm a body full of anxiety. I let fear nest itself in the back of my head. I'm an awkward and insecure mess, a body of bad choices at times. Heck, I even go hiking with nothing but basketball sneakers."

Mel giggled at that.

"Mel," I continued. "There's so much I want to apologize to you for, but honestly, I think apologies can only do so much. I don't want to say sorry just to do it again. I want to make a promise to you, that I'm going to do better, and that I'll hold myself accountable if I screw up."

"I'll hold you accountable, too." She grinned. "I should have told you sooner about my past, although that's not me apologizing. That's just me saying maybe things would have been a bit clearer."

"You definitely don't owe me an apology," I reassured her. "I was wrong, it was gross what I said, and I should have known better. You're amazing, you're beautiful, you're smart, funny, wise. You're like a song, but not like other songs, because other songs lose their magic when they get overplayed. But not you. You still make my heart race. Maybe I'm too young to know what love is, but this is the strongest I've ever felt toward anyone. Maybe this is better, maybe this is softer, maybe this is more honest. Maybe this is . . . I don't know," I rambled.

"No, I think you got it right." She squeezed my hand. "I think this might be the strongest I've ever felt for anyone, too. But if we do this, we need to build each other up. Not bring each other down."

She was right. Relationships are about growing together, and she was someone I wanted to grow with. If that required unlearning crappy behaviour, then I was all ears. I was ready for change. I was ready for Mel. I thought about what I had said to her in her bedroom, and how toxic it was. I had to tell her it wasn't true.

"You do care, y'know. It was wrong of me to say that. I

hope you know you're not as alone as you think," I told her.

"I know," she said. "I'm working on it. The whole opening myself up thing."

"There's no rush. Take it at your pace." I grinned.

"It's the only way I know how." She grinned back.

I wrapped my arms around her, still unsure if I should say it. I was thinking it, and it was on my mind the whole time, so I just said it.

"Melody, I love you."

The biggest smile made its way across her face, but she moved her head away in shyness.

"Shut up, beautiful boy." She turned her head back to me and gently touched my face with both of her hands, bringing me forward. Her lips met mine as she kissed me, and I closed my eyes. Her warmth filled my chest with what felt like magic. I finally felt like I was rebuilding the broken bridge between us. Mel was the song I wanted on replay, the person I wanted to have my back, and I wanted to have hers, too. I would, I promised her that.

"I love you, too," she said as she let go. I got closer and wrapped my arms around her waist. She laughed while she kissed my face. Mel made me feel a lot of things, but most importantly, she taught me that I'm worthy of love and happiness. Those were things that were often far away from my grasp, but now my heart felt as full as the moon.

Eventually we made our way inside the cabin. Mel had taken the keys from her dad. It wasn't very big on the inside. There was a couch, a bed, and a giant window that overlooked the lake. Mel opened up a trunk at the edge of the bed that had pillows and blankets inside. We made ourselves comfortable, and then she began tickling me, which led to a pillow fight, which then led to cuddling and lots more laughing, which led to conversation. We spoke about how we were going to help each other out, how we could build our relationship to a better place, and how we could support each other without dragging each other down. We were both very hopeful about it. I think the most important part of that night was that for the first time in a long time, we let ourselves be happy.

The next morning, I woke up while it was still early. I looked out the window of the cabin, and the stars were replaced with a purple sky and the sun trying to rise.

"Mel," I whispered. "Come see."

"Whaa?" she grumbled until she woke up. "What time is it?"

She grabbed her phone to check and said, "Shit, it's four-thirty in the morning."

She got out of bed and made her way to the window.

"Look at that," she observed.

"Yeah, look at that," I said as I put my arm around her and enjoyed the view. She grabbed my arm tight and smiled.

"Let's go for a drive," she suggested.

"I'm not opposed to that idea," I said. "Do we have to cross the river again?"

Mel smirked.

We travelled back to Mel's car, and both laughed when we got back to the river. We made it across. Together. We held hands the entire way with no intention of letting go. Once we got back to her car, she put her gunky boots in the truck and laughed at my ruined sneakers. I laughed, too.

I got in the passenger seat and she hopped in the driver's side, connected her AUX cord to her phone, and blasted it.

"Where are we going?" I asked. "I'm kinda hungry."

"You could use a bite to eat?"

"Yeah, yeah, I could." I smiled.

She smiled, too. "Let's find somewhere along the way."

"Where to?"

"Where ever that sky takes us," she said as she put the car into drive. She backed up on the dirt road and swerved around. I held on tight.

"Unless you have any objections?" she asked.

"You lead the way." I smiled.

"Then let's go." She hit the gas and drove off following the sky.

I was in love with her, and she loved me back. She gripped my hand tight, and we drove under the purple light that was fading the night away. Her melody brought me back from uncertainty and taught me how to see beauty, and somewhere along the distance of it all, I learned how to love. I learned to love honestly and openly, to wear my heart on my sleeve, and to also love myself even if I was full of faults. We didn't have a destination, but we didn't need one. The only thing we needed from each other was the reassurance of knowing that we weren't going to be alone. I didn't need the reassurance of a scale, or validation from anyone at school. I needed to focus on the people who cared about me. The Donnys, the Scarletts, the Mels.

Her hand was gripped around mine while the other was on the steering wheel. I knew we were in it together. I knew I could be honest and open, and I didn't have to hide anything from her. She didn't care how big or small I was. She loved me for who I was. My image didn't determine if I was worthy of love. Mel's hand wrapped around mine proved it. Her foot was on the gas, and I laid back in her passenger seat knowing that I would be okay. Knowing that I could handle it. Knowing that I could forgive myself. Knowing I would be forever thankful for her rhythms and her beats, knowing that I was forever thankful for Melody. My heart was heavy, but not with fear and anxiety anymore — it was full of love and support. It was a weight I could carry. Sure, people saw me as an inspiration, but I didn't want that burden. In truth, I was only lucky enough to be surrounded by people who brought out the best in me. They were the people that built me up while helping me unlearn my bad habits. They were the ones who continued to care even when I messed up. They were the ones who showed me support, the ones who made me, me. And the best part of it? They were the ones who helped me believe that I always was, and always will be, worthy of love.

# ACKNOWLEDGMENTS

I was a teenager when I first began writing this book. I knew very little about the world, although I knew that I had a story in my heart. While writing this book there were many late nights that broke into early mornings, many days where my mind drifted into the world I created, and lots of coffee to keep me afloat. I was lucky enough to be surrounded by individuals who inspired me to pursue this project even in the very early stages. This project would have never been where it is now if it wasn't for them. Here's a small list of folks I would like to thank: Wanda Lauren Taylor, who had really helped me shape the story from the beginning alongside the team at Formac Publishing. For Ashley Avery, who has motivated me while being a huge support during this entire process. I would also like to thank Jennifer Young for letting me ramble about all of my ideas. For Rebecca Thomas, who has helped me develop above average adulting skill while being a great mentor, and a great friend. For Georgia Konstantinidis, whose friendship has been timeless. For Angela Jorgensen, who has always believed in me. And for Morris Green, I still want to be you when I grow up.

MARQUIS

Québec, Canada